# GATHERED

# GATHERED

## KURT HANSEN

*To Debbie*

*Blessings!*

*Kurt Hansen*

*atmosphere press*

*To our ancestors,*
*With appreciation for the grace that has come*
*to us and through us.*

# PART ONE: AUTUMN

For man, autumn is a time of harvest, of gathering together.
For nature, it is a time of sowing, of scattering abroad.

Edwin Way Teale, *Autumn Across America (1956)*

# CHAPTER ONE

The leaves were starting their annual fashion show of decay a bit early this year, as the September morning roads of Chicago's outermost bounds succumbed again to the clutter of yellow school busses stopping and starting, crawling tractors toting farm implements, and frustrated commuters heading out for work in the city. On this first day of the new school year, the thick, forested hills were still mostly lush with late summer green, but the unmistakable metamorphosis had begun. Over the past fifteen years of living here, Sol noticed it was always a particular maple tree that led the way, turning suddenly bright red long before others showed any signs of fall. "Are you precocious? Or just tired of blending in..." Sol mused out loud. The tree didn't answer, but Amy did.

"Who are you talking to, Dad?"

"To the tree, I guess. I was talking to the tree."

Amy rolled her eyes in the dismissive manner of teenage girls everywhere and changed the subject to herself. "Don't forget to pick me up at Kelsey's tonight. We have play practice and then we're going to her house for pizza. Remember?"

"I remember," he said, still considering the maple among the oaks.

They arrived at Lancashire High School a bit ahead of time, remarkably, given the traffic. Amy gathered herself to leave, running a brush through her straw-blonde hair before hoisting her book bag as she grabbed the door handle. Sol put his hand on her shoulder, and she said, "What?" with an exasperated sigh. "Hey, Amy... you know I love you, right?"

Her face softened and she managed a coy, blushing smile that somehow communicated both little girl loving her daddy and grown woman leaving for her honeymoon all at once. "I know, Dad. I know. Don't forget. Kelsey's house." And out the door she went. Just like that. As though summer never happened at all. Just another day in the ever-unfolding possibility that was her life. Watching her, it occurred to Sol that the whole summer had passed, and he couldn't recall more than a few occasions of any meaningful time he had spent with her. *Did summer actually happen? Does she really know I love her? Does she even care?* When she entered the school without looking back at all, he felt strangely abandoned.

Someone tapped their horn behind him, and Sol pulled ahead, getting on with his day, too, but without the attendant sense of possibility. He surveyed the trees along the road as he disappeared into what he called the "metromess." All along the thirty-three miles into the western suburbs of Chicago he looked for more signs of the coming fall but found none. *Just another friggin' day.*

———

Once he arrived at work, Sol pulled into the parking garage, driving past the familiar names and expensive cars of those who had climbed highest up the Argenta corporate mountain. A. Miller, COO, drove a Lexus when he wasn't using the limo service, although he sometimes drove one of his two other cars, either of which cost three times the cost of Sol's. Mr. Miller even had a pre–World War II Duesenberg Phaeton, rumored to have once belonged to Hermann Goering, which he paid some professional restorer a fortune to fashion anew. He only took it out on special occasions, and never drove it in the city. Next in line was H. D. Melisson, Managing Director, who would never buy anything but a Mercedes Benz S Class, and was quite proud to say so at every possible opportunity.

Sol drove on, watching the automobile values decline relative to the perceived importance of each name in the company structure, until he reached his own parking spot, demarcated by a sign that read, "D. Solomon Severson III." The D was for Delbert, which he had always loathed, even if (or maybe because) it was both his grandfather's and father's name. But of course *Solomon* wasn't any better among all the Toms and Daves and Jimmys on the playground, so early on he preferred to be called Sol. Quite a handle on which to peg one's youthful identity but, like his parking space, it was what it was: a safe distance from any measure of social or professional import.

He exited the elevator on the fourteenth floor (really the thirteenth, but some architectural numerologist thought it best not to tempt fate) and headed down the hall to his office. His secretary, Emma Prentiss, rose from her desk as he approached.

"Good morning, Mr. Severson." It was a two-toned greeting, the higher tone accentuating the first word, offered with her usual bubbly élan.

"Good morning," he replied, taking the morning *Wall Street Journal* and *Chicago Sun Times* from her hand.

She followed him into his office. "You have a 10:00 with a Mr. James from Swift Co., lunch at 11:30 with your wife at Sevilla, and the accounting staff meeting in the board room at 2:00. You told me to remind you to bring..."

"Yes, yes," he interrupted her, "bring the fourth-quarter projections. I remember." Emma always seemed to enjoy just a bit too much her control of his day's activities.

"Coffee?" she asked.

"Yeah, and some orange juice, please."

"Right away, Mr. Severson," she replied, on her way out of the room. He buried himself in the business section of the *Times*.

Sol feigned brilliance in his meeting with James, who readily accepted the changes Sol suggested in his tax strategies. The man seemed genuinely agog at what, in Sol's mind, were relatively mundane adjustments. But since those adjustments would save him a crapload of money, Sol supposed agog was an appropriate response. And the appreciation was, well...appreciated.

Sol left for lunch with Jan, arriving before the place got crowded. Lorenz, the owner, greeted him with his usual gracious smile and hearty handshake. "Glad to see you again, Mr. Severson," he said, and seemed to mean it. Lorenz was one of those old-school restaurateurs who brought his family's generations-old Spanish recipes to this country, and who took great pride in the pleasure of his customers. You could see it in the laugh lines on his face and in the urgency with which he responded to any perceived desire of his customers. He also had one of the better wine cellars in the whole region.

"Sol?" Jan's voice called to him from the other end of the bar. He waved her over. They sat in the bar area and ordered tapas: a plate of little toasted breads with *tomate y anchoa*, some *calamari* in oil infused with garlic and basil, and *mancheco y jamon Iberica* topped with capers. Plus, the bread and olives that greeted diners at every table. And, of course, a couple glasses of a reasonable Tempranillo.

"Any drama from Amy this morning?" Jan asked

knowingly.

"Nope. No problems. She's off in her own little world. Too old to accept any real connection from dear old dad, and too young to realize she still needs it. I'm getting old."

"The circles they go 'round and 'round," Jan sang. She could still do a pretty good Joni Mitchell.

"How's things at the butcher shop?" he asked her. Jan worked as a surgical nurse for an orthopedic group at St. Joseph's Medical Center.

"Only two procedures. Kind of a slow day, especially for a Tuesday. But with school starting and just coming off the Labor Day weekend, I guess that's why. Had a total knee this morning with Dr. Dienst, and I'm scheduled for a hip replacement at 3:30 with Dr. Arpati, which is why you have to pick up Amy. Never know how much time those hips are gonna take." Jan saw Sol's eyes glazing over. He had sort of drifted away to thoughts of that red maple tree, for some crazy reason. "Are you still with me?"

"Yeah, of course," he said, not wanting to appear as disinterested as he was feeling inside. Truth is, he didn't give much of a damn what went on at the hospital, so long as he didn't have to be there. He always hated hospitals. He even hated hospital shows on TV. Too much drama.

They finished their afternoon diversion and went their separate ways. Back at the office, Sol prepared for his part of the staff meeting, glad to be able to offer a rosy outlook in the upcoming fourth quarter. Not that anyone actually believed the statistical inferences, but if you have to *appear* to believe something, it might as well be something positive.

The day wore on to its inevitable conclusion, and as he walked past Emma's desk to head home, she saw him glance up at the plethora of family photos decorating both her desk and the wall behind her. "Some new pictures, I see." She looked up and said, "I have a lot of family. We love getting together, so there's always more pictures."

It was an impressive menagerie, that's for sure. But Sol sensed she was about to start identifying everyone, so he turned down the hall. "Well, nice pictures. See you tomorrow, Emma," he said, hoping he had masked his relief at escaping. He didn't wish to offend his secretary, but he had never had much patience for family gatherings. In the seventeen years he and Jan had been married, Jan had been happy to keep track of birthdays and anniversaries, and she even liked sending out Christmas cards with a family letter chronicling their year's events (*as though anyone really cared*). And for his part, Sol was always glad she wanted to do it, because if he had to do the corresponding, everyone would think they had died or gone into witness protection.

As he once again joined the "metromess," Sol began looking forward to relaxing with a scotch and water with his feet up and maybe some music. Maybe Joni, *Ladies of the Canyon. The Circle Game*. "Crap!" he said out loud. Amy at Kelsey's. He rigorously avoided drinking and driving (especially with Amy in the car), so he would forego the scotch; but the realization made him surly. He even forgot to look for the maple tree. Another day in the life of a successful suburbanite father in greater Chicagoland.

When he got home, he walked into the kitchen as usual, and he noticed the message light blinking on the answering machine. He decided to ignore it. No scotch? No message. Screw it.

So now what to do? On his way up the drive Sol noticed

a few leaves had begun to gather on the lawn near the street. Although it seemed premature, he decided to kill some time by raking them up. He got the rake and a lawn-waste bag out of the garage and headed out, stopping along the way just to admire the quiet. A soft breeze wafted from the west, and Sol closed his eyes for a moment, leaning on his rake. *Peaceful*, he thought. *Life ought to be more peaceful.*

He moved over to where the smattering of leaves had caught his attention and began to move them into a pile. An older gentleman approached, walking his Sheltie tethered with a retractable leash. Sol looked up, anticipating some conversation. The man walked by without any acknowledgment at all. Sol felt wounded, as though he had been snubbed. The man certainly had seen Sol, but he kept his gaze staunchly set ahead. It was as if he was determined *not* to see Sol. So, Sol did what he often did: he created an address in his mind, a speech he imagined himself delivering. *Well, good day to you, too, Mr. Perfect! I hope your dog bites you in the ankle, and it gets infected, and you have to go to the hospital, and nobody comes to see you there, and even the nurses won't talk to you.*

Sol finished up his raking chore and headed back in to the garage, leaf bag in tow, feeling amused at his little imaginary diatribe, but also discouraged and alone.

He picked up Amy on schedule, and on returning he was surprised to see Jan's Prius in the garage. Apparently, it had been a quick hip replacement. As they walked into the kitchen, Jan inquired about the play practice. "It went fine," Amy replied automatically before retreating to her bedroom refuge.

"There's a message on the answering machine from your Aunt Christine. Your Uncle George died. She wants you to call her right away. I wrote down the number."

Sol's first inclination was to respond, "So what?" He remembered Uncle George fondly from his younger years in Wisconsin, but he had become so detached from his family in the past twenty or so years, that Uncle George's passing seemed as affecting as that of a casual acquaintance whose obituary he might have happened upon in the paper. *So-and-so died. Hmm. Turn the page...*

But Sol dialed the number and soon heard the distantly familiar voice of his Aunt Christine. He tried to sound compassionate and concerned. "Yes, I remember. I was fond of him, too. I'm sure it must be very hard to lose him... The funeral is next Wednesday morning? Of course, I'll be there," he heard himself saying. He found the button on the phone marked "End" and pushed it.

———————————

Sol planned to take off the coming Tuesday and Wednesday, but the next several days found Sol increasingly pensive. When he arrived at work on Monday and exited the elevator, Sol was truly dreading the sound of Emma's cheery repartee. He walked right past her and into his office. She soon followed him in, but he interrupted her before she began, "Nothing this morning, thanks." She sensed his mood and replied, "I'll be at my desk if you need anything." He responded with silence, his eyes fixed on some piece of paper he wasn't actually reading.

Later that morning he had a meeting with two board members from St. Justin's nursing home. Jim Barnes, a local attorney, and Sister Mary Thomas, the administrator of the home, were seeking advice on how they might address an anticipated cash-flow problem. Normally Sol would have studied the issue ahead of time, but when Emma buzzed to announce his guests' arrival, the moment came upon him like a surprise. Sol suddenly realized he had not given their concerns any thought at all. A sudden wave of anxiety surged from his lower back into his abdomen and moved upward, like a vise gripping his chest. He thought for a minute he might faint. He even thought his heart might be seizing, and for a fleeting second, he saw himself in a coffin, at a funeral home, with Jan and Amy crying amidst the flowers and potted plants.

Sol stood and shook himself – literally – and forced himself to focus on the problem at hand. It was a skill he had developed early on, the ability to push back whatever he might be feeling and focus instead on something which he could fix. He responded to Emma, "Offer them some refreshments and have them sit in the reception area. I'll be with them in a little bit." He opened up the St. Justin's file that Emma had faithfully left on his desk, and he reviewed their most recent budget review and investment profile. He could see the coming cash-flow problem and, just as quickly, he saw a possible solution involving a municipal bond, which, if cashed out, would cover the situation nicely. He invited the board members in, and in fifteen minutes they left satisfied. *I did it again,* he thought to himself. *I fooled everyone into believing I'm brilliant.*

———

Tuesday morning did finally arrive, but not before Sol had suffered a restless night. He was not looking forward to the six-hour drive to Tomah. He left Tomah after college over twenty years ago and had only gone back a couple of times for the holidays until his dad died, followed soon after by his mother, so there'd been little to draw him back to Tomah. Until now. He hoped his sister, Maura, might make it back for the funeral, but he doubted it. Maura, married and living in Ohio, was even less connected to the family than he was.

Sol took I-90 northwest toward Wisconsin. The developing autumn foliage progressed further with every hour of the route. *Fall really was coming,* he thought to himself. And soon after, Thanksgiving and the whole Christmas market craze. The desperate retailers had begun finding ways to cash in on the annual buying spree earlier and earlier, using the sensible-sounding notion of layaway as the frame in which to slip some Christmassy images. *Get 'em while they're hot and make 'em as hot as you can.* Christmas trees standing alongside the shelves of Halloween candy. It made Sol bristle with tired cynicism.

The miles piled up, the traffic constant but manageable. So many trucks! All those goods moving along at 75 miles an hour. By the time he pulled into the Holiday Inn Express at Tomah, he was ready for a steak, a good scotch, and a bed, and after texting Jan, he located those very things, and in that order.

# CHAPTER TWO

"Sol!" His mother was calling him for the fifth or sixth time to come in for dinner. He had learned (by watching the men of the family) that Nordic, cautious reluctance to come to the table which characterized most of the Severson men (and infuriated those who prepared their food). It was somehow unmasculine to appear too eager to eat, and especially so when gathered with others at a special meal like Thanksgiving or a birthday party. The more special the occasion it seemed, the more reluctance was due. He never understood it, but he had adopted the tradition. Even when he was truly hungry, twelve-year-old Sol was a Severson in the making. He would delay the affair until the cook became just irate enough. Then he'd go.

Affinity with his father and uncles would have been a good enough reason to dawdle, but his current reluctance came from the perfect laziness of the day, and the kingdom over which he reigned in his own backyard. As he sat under the big maple tree, the cool breeze on his face moderated the warmth of the slowly receding sun, and the smell of newly mown grass intoxicated him with late summer indolence. He'd been out there all afternoon (after he'd finished mowing the lawn), sometimes reading from his favorite book, *The Adventures of Huckleberry Finn*, sometimes dozing off, and most of the time simply letting his mind wander.

The sky was so blue it seemed unlikely, yet there it was. And right beside him the big, black ants moved in deliberation, exiting and entering their huge, sandy nest, apparently unaware or unconcerned that this enormous creature, this adolescent god-human who had the power to crush and destroy them at his whim, was hovering inches away, intently watching their every move. *I am Sol, king of the universe. I can destroy you, if I choose.*

"Delbert Solomon Junior! Get in here for supper or I'll give it to the dog! And tell your sister to come in, too."

His mother's words broke through his reverie. He always hated it when she called him by his full name. And he especially hated it when she referred to him as "Junior." Kings of universes shouldn't get called names like "Junior." Neither should they be required to fetch annoying siblings. "How should I know where the little twerp is?" he shouted back with a lordly irritation.

"She's next door at Twila's." Maura and Twila spent much of their free time together, most of it watching cartoons on the Schmidts' big television in their family room downstairs. "Now get up and get going! I mean it!!"

There was that tone. Time to move toward the food. One last survey of the ant world under his sovereign domain, and then Sol got up and went to find Maura. He hopped the fence with ease, and noticed his mother watching from the kitchen window. Her look of admiration at his physical prowess made him blush a little, but he walked just a bit faster in hopes she might not see.

The back door flew open and the kids came bounding in just as Sol's mother put the potatoes and Swiss steak and the steaming, formerly frozen peas on the table.

"Shut up, twerp!"

"No, you shut up, you big jerk!"

"Zit-face!"

"Greaseball!"

"Ass-wipe!"

"Sol, that's enough!!" his mother ordered. "What kind

of language is that to use in this house? Wait till your father gets home. He will not be pleased, I can tell you that!"

At least she had called him Sol. He flopped into his chair at the table, grabbing for the meat platter, and with a sidelong glance, he noticed the chair at the head of the table, empty as usual. The empty chair offered a hollow support to his mother's threats. Sol's father was often away on business for a week or more at a time, a reality to which the family had grown accustomed, and one which altered his function in the family's life. In his absence, the family operated without him, but differently, referring to him only by allusion. And on his return, the family seemed centered on him, as though his renewed presence among them precluded all other matters.

Whatever had happened in the days when Sol's father was gone hadn't necessarily very much to do with him, even when he was home. Sol had come to learn that the accumulated transgressions, for which he was promised later punishment at the hands of the absent man, often piled up in that empty chair and then evaporated when the real man came to sit in it. In those years of adolescent power-brokerage, such keen knowledge of how things worked brought Sol a measure of ownership and mastery. Later – much later – when he would think back on those times at home, it would be with a hollow feeling which he could not explain.

Of course, the most egregious misdeeds would not go unpunished. Sol had learned by now how to differentiate minor and grievous misdeeds, and he dared not offend his father too much, even in absentia. Like the time he had stolen a candy bar from the grocery store. He was thirteen years old, and his friend, Tim, had dared him to do it. While

Sol had a moral center of sorts (he had, in fact, attended Sunday school), a dare was a dare. And, if the truth be told, he harbored a secret thrill at the prospect of the nefarious undertaking. He just had to see if he could really get away with it.

They planned it out, he and Tim. They would ride their bikes to the little mom-and-pop grocery store and park them at opposite ends of the building. They would walk in and go directly to the back of the store, where the milk and cheese were kept. It would be normal looking, just like two kids who were sent by their mom to get a gallon of milk. They thought about wearing dark glasses and baseball caps to hide their identities, but Nora, the checkout girl (the youngest, though grown, daughter of Ray and Evelyn Kohler, the mom and pop who owned the store), would know them anyway, and they didn't want to call undue attention to themselves. Caps, but no sunglasses, they decided.

When the day came, they met at Tim's house. "You ready?" Tim challenged.

"Ready."

"Sure you won't chicken out?" Tim's words cemented the deal.

"Not me. Let's go." They rode off together with an air of excitement as yet unimagined, at least by Sol, who, by the time they got to the store, felt his heart pounding almost as hard as after he ran the half-mile in gym class. They parked their bikes at either end of the place, just like they planned. To make their getaway, they would take off in different directions and meet up back at Sol's house. *Divide, misdirect, confuse...* As they walked up to the entrance of the little neighborhood grocery, Sol thought he heard a guitar playing the theme from James Bond in the background: *Dohm ditta dohm-dohm, dohm-dohm. Dohm ditta dohm-dohm, dohm-dohm.*

They walked to the back of the store. *Normal. Just try to look normal*, he kept thinking, not having the slightest clue what normal looked like to the casual observer. They walked around to the side aisle where the candy was kept. *Damn!* Nothing but big packages of candy bars, six to a box! No way to conceal a big package like that (although the thought of stealing six candy bars brought a moment of elation, accompanied by roughly six times the anxiety). *No! You have to be realistic. One candy bar can be done. You must complete your mission!* But the only single candy bars were up front, right by the check-out lane and right in front of the all-seeing eyes of Nora the checkout girl.

Sol grabbed Tim and pushed him back toward the milk cooler. "You have to get her attention while I grab the candy," Sol whispered with urgency.

"I-I-I never said I'd help you," Tim said, backpedaling. "You said you could do this. Or maybe you really *are* just a chickenshit!" The gauntlet had been thrown down, and Sol unflinchingly picked it up. He shoved Tim toward the front of the store, waiting for the right opportunity.

Nora had just finished sacking up old Mrs. Jackson's groceries, and was helping her get her three bags into the little wire basket pull-behind cart she always brought to the market. That's when Sol saw his chance. He grabbed the first candy bar he could get his hands on and shoved it deep into the pocket of his jacket. *Mission accomplished!* He left the store quickly (*Normal! Look normal!*) and mounted his bike. The James Bond theme now twanged in his head, accompanied by the triumphant, blaring trumpets

announcing his fait accompli: *Ta-dum, ta-Da, ta-Da-Da!*
*007 climbs into his Aston Martin, ready to drive through*
*the Alps and make a clean getaway, having accomplished*
*his mission, left his enemies in utter shame, and the*
*beautiful blonde whatshername bereft and heartbroken,*
*pleading with him to stay.*

A woman's voice broke through his vaunted
imaginings. "Just a minute, Sol!" It was the same tone his
mother used to call him to the table. A moment later,
Evelyn Kohler had him by the scruff of his jacket. She
pulled on him with a tight grip, yanking him right off the
back of his bike. His jacket slid up his shoulder, and the
Reese's peanut butter cup in its bright orange wrapper fell
onto the parking lot. Sol heard Tim's tires spinning off the
gravel as he rode off, leaving Sol to suffer his fate alone.
And somehow, he knew even at that moment that this time
his father *would* get involved.

All week he relived the scene, waiting for his dad's
return. The shameful walk back into the store. The phone
call to his mother. The long, lonely ride back home (*where*
*was Tim now, the little weasel?*) to his glaring mother,
standing on the front porch with arms crossed. The hours
spent after school in his room, day after day, awaiting his
doom. It was how he imagined death row might be.
*What're you in for? Peanut butter cup.*

When his father did return, it was almost a relief.
Almost. The fact that Sol was grounded for two weeks, and
that he had to go back to the store owner and make a
formal apology, along with an offer to do work at the store
for a week after school with no pay, all this seemed
somehow to make the whole thing feel better. But it was
the look in his father's eyes that he could not escape – that

look of utter disappointment and melancholy as he shook his head, looking at the floor. And worse than that look were his words: "You have brought shame to this family." Daggers could not have hurt more than those words. The lesson stayed with him: some things you just don't do. And some things, once done, can't be undone.

Sol disliked remembering his failings. But his father's empty chair had a way of inviting those memories. When his father was home, filling that chair, the conversation could be about anything – school or sports trivia, things that happened on his business trip, or things they might be planning to do together as a family. But when Del Severson was away, that empty chair spoke loudly and with dispatch. All Sol could think of were the various ways he had never measured up, and never could. That chair was his accuser, judge, and punisher, unmasking his sins through an unwelcome but unavoidable confession. Maybe that's why Sol ate so quickly.

He finished his steak and potatoes, disregarding the peas. He cleared his place as usual, walking past the empty chair, through the kitchen and eventually upstairs to the sanctuary of his bedroom. Closing the door behind him, he began to feel once again the safety and peace of his own place in the world, small and insignificant as it was. There, on his bed, he sank once more into the boyhood saga of Huck Finn, where he remained until he fell asleep.

# CHAPTER THREE

Sol sat with the others in the small country church on the hill in rural Monroe County. They were there to pay last respects to George Anders Severson, the older brother of Sol's father, Delbert Solomon Severson, Jr. *How strange to be here,* Sol thought to himself. *Without Maura here, it's only me and Aunt Christine left, and we have nothing in common. Yet here we are, just like when Dad and Mom died. We're like turkey buzzards, feasting on the dead.*

"A reading from the beloved Psalm 23: The Lord is my shepherd; I shall not be in want.." the pastor continued. But it all seemed a bit ludicrous. It seemed to Sol that everyone in the place was in want. His uncle George, lying there in his best brown suit, wanted to be alive. His wife, Christine, wanted him to be alive, too, although if pressed, she probably couldn't have put two sentences together to explain why. Like most of the Severson family, George and Christine had lived their married life out in a measure of years. They raised twin sons, Sol's cousins Jake and Joseph, who were three years older than Sol, and who both died tragically in a car crash at age seventeen. George and Christine somehow survived this terrible loss, and when George began his flirtations in mid-life, Christine had settled for a route of least resistance instead of taking him to the cleaners.

All the others in attendance, too, wanted for something. As a group of individual souls, they probably could have filled Fort Knox with the sum total of their wanton wantingness. And as it rattled in the space between Sol's ears, the pastor's funeral message wanted for something, too. Sol couldn't help but chuckle to himself: *it's a message for the dead, delivered to the dead, by the dead.* It seems no one was exempt from being in want, least of all, D. Solomon Severson III.

As the comforting message bathed the ears of the polite, uncomfortable hearers, he surveyed the little sanctuary. The church itself was charming, in its way. Typical of country churches in Wisconsin, the interior was immaculately kept. A hand-carved, white altar of ornate styling was trimmed with gold paint, reminiscent of its truly gilded past. There was a white and gold communion rail which reached out in a semi-circle from the altar, with a matching white and gold ambo, elevated slightly above the nave. A white and gold baptismal font sat off to one side. A worn, but clean, red carpet joined the main aisle with an intersecting front walkway leading to the outside aisles, and on the one side to the fellowship hall and pastor's office. In the classic design of church architecture, the aisles formed a cross, which was more apparent if you climbed the stairs to the balcony.

The pews were old, handmade from the days when local folks had the time and talent and inclination to hand-make such things for their church. Constructed of hewn oak, the pews were darkly stained and shined with multiple coats of varnish that had been applied and reapplied over the years to protect aging wood from the grasping insults of new, grubby little hands. As each person found their spot for the service, the pews creaked and groaned, perhaps revealing the cost of the many years supporting the weight of the faithful.

The windows were absolutely beautiful. Each window space was in the shape of an apse, and each displayed a stained-glass scene of a different biblical story. As the sun streamed through the ornate creations, Sol was surprised at how readily he recognized and remembered the stories depicted there. On the side where he sat, the window farthest from the front showed Jesus feeding the 5,000, and the next one was a clear image of Jesus delivering the Sermon on the Mount. Then there was a depiction of Jesus appearing with Elijah and Moses in the Transfiguration, and in another there was Jesus calming the stormy sea. There were similar depictions in all the windows on the other side of the sanctuary, and Sol could identify every one. *Those Sunday school days really must have made an impression*, he thought to himself. It had been many years since he had been to church or spent any time at all reading the Bible, but the stories leapt out of the stained glass and retold themselves to him as he sat there. It was a little unnerving. And maybe a little humbling.

No one could afford such artistry as this today, especially a little church in the country. And he noticed the little brass plaques beneath each window: "Donated in memory of Ella Skogsrud," "Donated in memory of Lars and Carrie Carlsson," "Donated in memory of Knud Thorvaldson." *All those old Scandinavian farmers, giving to their posterity in death what they couldn't afford to enjoy for themselves in life*, he thought. He appreciated their generosity.

And despite himself, Sol began feel an uncharacteristic sense of connectedness. These were his roots. Those old Scandinavian farmers had formed the community from which he had emerged. And while he found little comfort among these relative strangers, Sol was surprised by the comfort he found in the place itself.

"Let us pray," the pastor invited. "O God, your days are

without end and your mercies cannot be counted. Make us aware of the shortness and uncertainty of human life, and let your Holy Spirit lead us in holiness and righteousness all the days of our life, so that, when we shall have served you in our generation, we may be gathered to our ancestors, having the testimony of a good conscience, in the communion of your church, in the confidence of a certain faith, in the comfort of a holy hope, in favor with you, our God, and in peace with all humanity; through Jesus Christ our Lord. Amen."

It was a good prayer. Something about it stuck with Sol, gave him peace and a sense of belonging, something his life had been lacking, though he hadn't been able to put a finger on it. *"Gathered to our ancestors,"* he thought to himself. The phrase repeated like a refrain in his head the rest of the day. Through all the pleasant, banal claptrap of reacquainting and storytelling among the mourners at the funeral lunch (which, following interment, was served in the church basement by several graying members of the parish ladies guild), those words kept reasserting themselves. Even in the six hours it took to drive back home afterward, the words returned: *gathered to our ancestors...*

---

The drive back to Chicago was like traveling through time. After all these years living away from Tomah, the return to life in suburban Chicago seemed surreal. Like paisley laid over chintz, some things just don't fit together; even if the colors match, the textures don't.

As he made his way through the predictable traffic snarls to his adopted hometown of Oakton Lakes, Sol was struck by the excruciating sameness of it all. All the homes so manicured and perfect. On their street, nothing had been built under 2,500 square feet (a neighborhood association minimum), and most were substantially larger. The neighborhood association required every home to have a brick facade, and it prohibited fences. A casual glance would reveal perfect trees, perfect lawns, perfect everything, and all at a perfectly audacious price. The neighborhood association made sure of it. *Neighborhood! That's a joke!* he thought. *This was no neighborhood, not like in Tomah.*

Driving down the highway, Sol's mind began to drift back to the neighborhood of his youth, which consisted of people who knew one another, idiosyncrasies and all. There was Mr. Palmer, an old widower who lived in the upper flat of the Johnson house, two doors down at 1727½ Elm St. Old Mr. Palmer was a neighborhood fixture. Every day after school, Sol and his sister would depart the school bus at the end of the block and walk past all the houses on the street, and there would be Mr. Palmer, sitting in his chair on the balcony of his apartment (which was really the flat front-porch roof). He always wore a sleeveless T-shirt, at least in the warmer months, and he always had his glass of "tea" on the little rusted, white wrought-iron table beside him. Sol learned much later that the "tea" was really Jack Daniels with just enough water to make it appear the color of tea, and that old Mr. Palmer was a life-long alcoholic, which explained some of his oddness, but probably not all of it.

The Johnsons, from whom old Mr. Palmer rented his flat, were a nice, older couple who mostly kept to themselves. They had raised what some would call a "passel" of kids – eight in all. It was a regular occurrence to see one or several of the grandkids – the progeny of the passel – being deposited at Grandma and Grandpa's for safekeeping, while the adult children variously worked or played. One had the sense that Mrs. Johnson's fatigue and joy in child-rearing had amalgamated into the aggregate definition of her existence, while Mr. Johnson spent a good deal of his time out fishing. Every year, Christmas Eve was quite the affair at the Johnson house. All the children and grandchildren came to eat a meal and open presents, and the backyard, front yard, both sides of the street and even the alleyway took on the appearance of a used car lot.

Old Mr. Palmer had a counterpart, though much younger and with a more ignoble reputation, who lived across the street on the corner at 1732½ Elm. His name was Steve Genovese, and he rented the flat directly above his parents' home – some said because he still needed their supervision, even at age thirty-something. Steve kept to himself, but he could sometimes be seen roaming the streets and skulking around the neighborhood's old, three-story school building in the wee hours. Rumors abounded about Steve; how he had been a hit man for the mob in Chicago (a scenario derived from the Italian surname, no doubt); how he had been in a mental institution after killing someone; that he was a homosexual and a communist; and the most fantastic (and certainly most likely): that he had been discovered torturing and ultimately killing the neighborhood cats after a couple dozen feline corpses were found atop a local warehouse roof with ropes tied around their necks. Sol and Maura were always cautioned by their mother to stay away from Steve Genovese, whom the local kids referred to with trepidation as "Creepy Crawler."

The Schmidts lived next door at 1729 Elm. Mr. Schmidt was an auto parts dealer in downtown Tomah, and his wife, Ellie, was what they referred to in those days as a "homemaker," just like Sol's mother. Ellie grew some of the most wonderful flower gardens in the neighborhood, and the Schmidt lawn was the finest in the whole block. Never a dandelion, not in the Schmidt's grass (which also had the effect of prompting both the Johnson and Severson families to put forth more effort in lawn care than either family might otherwise have done). Eldon and Ellie Schmidt had four children: Allen, Tina, Donald, and Maura's friend, Twila. There was always a sense of balance in the lives of the Schmidts, although it was accompanied by a kind of ephemeral quality, as though what you were seeing was never quite completely accurate, even if it was socially acceptable and worthy of admiration.

Across the street and up a couple houses at 1720 Elm lived Mr. and Mrs. Sanchez. Albert had come originally from Mexico City to work in the fields, but he met a local girl, Doris Evertsen, at a Catholic church social. Doris' family had not approved of her choice for a husband, and it was told that even many years later, Albert was still not welcome at her grandmother's house. After twenty years of marriage, they remained childless (old Grandma Evertsen said this was God's punishment on Doris), but Doris and Albert doted on all the kids on the block. There were always extra treats on Halloween at the Sanchez house. Some kids actually went and changed costumes in order to reap the Sanchez candy harvest a second or even third time.

Sol could remember them all, and even many more, like Raymond, the kid born with hydrocephalus, who mostly hung around in his wheelchair and talked incessantly about his girlfriend (whom no one had ever seen, and who almost certainly existed only in Raymond's fantasies). But Sol hadn't thought about any of them for a very long time. As he revisited his boyhood neighborhood in his mind, the colors of the houses and the colorfulness of the people all came flowing back with a comforting and startling ease. They were a veritable palette of people, all living in proximity, and all blendable with the brush strokes of memory, melded by their shared history into a broad panorama, much like the color-rich autumn trees.

As he wound his way through the unnecessarily curving streets of Oakton Lakes, Sol was struck by the disparity between what he was remembering and the life he had come to know. *Neighborhood!* he scoffed. *These people wouldn't know a neighborhood if it walked up and shook their hand! Which would never happen. Probably forbidden by the Neighborhood Association.*

*Association! That's another joke!* Sol thought. Despite the lack of fences, none of the inhabitants of Oakton Lakes associated at all. He remembered that back in Tomah, neighbors talked across the backyard fence, invited each other to come in for a drink or for dinner, and had backyard cookouts with kids from several families running around. There was even an annual block party.

Once a year, they would obtain a permit from the police department to block off the entrance and exit to the 1700 block of Elm St., and folks would bring out grills and coolers and set up games in the street and on the lawns, and the kids would be entertained by Mr. Simpson, who had a clown costume, and after the sun set low and the kids were all worn down and placed safely in their beds, the adults would sit around drinking cokes or beer or coffee, and they would talk and play sheep's head or cribbage until 1:00 or 2:00 a.m. Neighbors in Sol's memory not only associated, they *lived* together.

But not here. Here in this affluent sub-division of the affluent suburb of Chicago, the affluent sub-neighbors had adopted a sub-definition of associating, which simply meant they agreed to certain parameters regarding the houses they built. The end result was that everything looked pretty much uniform. In the back of his mind, he heard Malvina Reynolds' mocking, sardonic voice: *and they're all made out of ticky-tacky and they all look just the same.*

Sol sighed aloud, a sad, lonesome sigh. As he surveyed the well-landscaped properties unfolding one after another before him, he was caught in a sudden well of emptiness which almost overwhelmed him. *These people are no more alive than old Uncle George!* he thought, almost out loud. *They ought to change the name of the so-called Neighborhood Association. They ought to call it the Pact of Uniformity! P. U.!*

His customary cynicism was returning. It was familiar, if unhelpful. He turned into the driveway of 12809 Oakmont, with the red-brick columns by the street which matched the red-brick front of the house (as required by P. U.), and pushed the appropriate numbers on the digital security system, resulting in the lights going on and the garage door opening to his customary place. He drove the Honda up to the exact spot in the garage, to that precise spot where his car door could open without hitting either the garage wall or the carefully arranged stuff stored on the wall. He had even hung a tennis ball from the ceiling on a string at just the perfect place to guide the driver to that spot. And on arriving perfectly again at that perfect spot, he switched off the engine and pushed the button to close the garage door.

Sol sat there in his car, safe in the cocoon of his garage, and he wondered: *Do these so-called neighbors feel as lonely and empty as me? Maybe emptiness is the inevitable outcome for a bunch of Neighborhood Association members who don't know what a neighborhood is and who don't know how to associate.*

His analysis brought him little comfort. In the rearview mirror, the outside world receded, and the garage door clicked shut. Everything was in its place, including that notable member of the wanting Severson diaspora, D. Solomon the Third. *Home sweet home.*

# CHAPTER FOUR

Jan Severson lay in her cozy bed, under her warm, down comforter, reading the latest novel from Oprah's book club. Deep as she was in the role of the current heroine protagonist, Jan barely noticed the sound of the garage door. And when she heard Sol's familiar rustlings in the kitchen, through the family room and on to the hallway that led to their bedroom, she anticipated his emergence with a bit of dread. Not only was she not wishing to detach herself from the plot of her book, she wished even less to attach herself to the world of Sol's family in Tomah, and she knew when he walked through that door she would have to do just that. She had deftly avoided the trip to Uncle George's funeral with a well-timed work obligation, although if she thought Sol really needed her, she could easily have taken the time off. But she didn't want to.

Jan always felt uncomfortable with Sol's family, a feeling which became even more intense as she learned how uncomfortable Sol himself was with his family. She and Sol had built a life together in a completely different world from the folksy, small-town existence of Tomah, Wisconsin, and as the years and the life experiences piled up into a personal history of their own, she found they increasingly lacked a language to enable much, if any, connection at all to the people of Sol's past and their world. This vagueness, this disconnection, seemed not to be a problem for Sol until and unless he had occasion to reconnect with his family, such as his Uncle George's funeral had provided today. So, as Sol came through the bedroom door, that empty lostness was there on his face. She knew it would be. That's what she was dreading.

"Hi, honey." She managed to sound inviting.

"Hey. You're looking your usual part." He loved seeing her tucked in bed, reading, her shoulder-length blondish hair tousled a bit by the pillows propping her up. Jan never agreed with Sol's assessment that she was beautiful, but Sol didn't need her agreement. He fell in love with her almost as soon as he saw her. Her then very blonde hair, straight and originally long in the manner of the '70s; her smallish, perfectly shaped breasts; her long, strong legs and tiny feet. He was initially so enrapt by her beauty that he avoided her, fearing she would reject him outright. But when he overcame his reluctance, she accepted his invitation. Coffee and a walk. That's how it began. And after getting past her physical beauty, he learned to love even more the person he came to know.

Jan broke away from her book, watching as Sol emptied his pockets in front of the dresser. His light brown hair was neatly trimmed, as usual. He had always been fit, and his rather strong shoulders were still appealing to Jan, especially when his back was turned to her. He removed his jacket and hung it in the closet, revealing the thick hair on his forearms. When he emerged from the bathroom, he removed the remainder of his clothing down to his boxer shorts, and he sat on the bed beside her. He leaned down to kiss her. It was the kind of kiss that can only lead to more kissing.

Jan was surprised but pleased to love away the lostness rather than having to talk about it. They made love that evening with a rare passion born of spontaneity and urgency.

Afterward, Sol turned toward her and covered her with his arm, pulling her close. *Here it comes*, she thought. *Here comes the lostness.* "I sure was glad to get back home," he began. "But as I was driving, I couldn't help noticing the difference again. How different everything is now. I don't know why, but it all seemed kind of empty. You ever feel that way?"

Jan didn't answer. Instead, she focused on keeping her breath deep and steady, as if she were asleep. What a question. Of course, she felt empty at times. But she had learned – painfully – not to succumb to the emptiness, how to survive by filling it up. She couldn't afford to let Sol's emptiness reconnect her with her own. So, she feigned sleep. And soon the pretense became the reality.

Sol looked over at Jan's hair laying over her slim shoulders. Watching her breathe, he began to recall the earlier times before her nursing career when she was practicing law. She was brilliant. And so focused! Her ability to stay focused served her well throughout law school, earning her magna cum laude graduation and an invitation to the *Law Review*. And in the tough world of corporate law, that same focus had made her the envy of her peers and the darling of her superiors. She rose through the ranks toward full partnership at Jennings, Jennings, and Albright – one of the most prestigious law firms in greater Chicago – faster than anyone previously had.

But the focus came at a cost. Jan had to learn the hard way what that old cliché about being "lost in your work" really meant. She could get so focused, so driven to succeed in her work that her availability to anything and everything else – and everyone, as well – became compromised. The result was loneliness and a bout with severe depression which eventually cost her the career she worked so hard to build, and almost cost her the marriage she had waited too long to enjoy.

After the medication, a sabbatical leave, and psychotherapy, it became apparent Jan needed a different career. She went back to school to train as a nurse. Being bright, she accomplished what most would deem a radical change in a short three years. It was a good move; she was much more balanced now. And along the way, she discovered her need to read. Regularly. Voraciously, even. Like sunlight to a plant, Jan needed the enlightenment and psychic nourishment of a well-written fiction to enable and ennoble the nonfiction of her own story.

Which was why Sol found it so comforting to find her there in bed, reading. The memory of those days when Jan was so troubled and lost was horrible for him. And although he hoped for more from her after his sad trip home from Tomah, he realized he had gotten what support she could give him. Sol kissed Jan lightly on the shoulder, and then turned over to face his emptiness alone.

# CHAPTER FIVE

When the sunlight peeked through the slats of the window shade, Sol was dreaming. He and his father were puttering a fishing boat down the Des Plaines River through the Loop of downtown Chicago, surrounded by all the traffic noise, the towering glass, and glinting steel. Sol had hooked a fish, but when he looked up to his dad, the scene changed. He was back on Lake Tomah, and it was his friend Tim with him in the boat and Tim was catching the fish.

He stood up to complain, "Hey, that was my fish!" Sudden fear gripped him as he felt the boat begin to capsize in slow motion. He felt himself falling overboard, and then the water cascading over him and the darkness below pulling him down. He struggled with all his might to get back to the light and to the boat, but it was like trying to swim in mud. The bleak panic of facing death nearly overwhelmed him, and as he looked up, he realized he was looking again at the skyline of Chicago. He was back in the Des Plaines River, and all around him the water was on fire! And worst of all, his dad was guiding their little boat away, seemingly unaware of Sol's presence there in the flaming water. Sol called out to him, but his father couldn't hear him. He drove the boat away, looking very sad and gloomy.

When Sol woke up, the bed linens were twisted around his arm and his waist like a cotton fetter. He was drenched with sweat, and the wetness of his body further confused him, delaying a bit longer his escape from the dream-river to the safe, dry Thursday morning of reality. He sat on the edge of the bed, trying to get his bearings. *Just a crazy dream. Dreams don't have to mean anything. Forget it.*

As Sol welcomed the steamy spray of the shower, he recalled a time early in his marriage. They were still living in Tomah in an apartment owned by one of his dad's suppliers, back when he and Jan were both working on their college degrees at the University of Wisconsin-La Crosse, his in accounting and hers in pre-law political science. The memory was so intense it was like watching a movie.

"You'll be wanting sex now," she said matter-of-factly. Like the dirt clods and little bits of dried cow shit on the back porch leading to the barn, which could have been but never were swept away, she had drawn her conclusion. Her name was Nellie Schuman, and Sol had just finished fixing the screen door on that back porch, a door which had for some time hung uselessly, like the rucksack that drooped from a rusty nail in the wall beside the doorway.

They were not and never had been lovers, only neighbors, and not even neighbors really, but business acquaintances. Back then, Sol did handyman work in the summers and on weekends to help with the cost of school, and ever since her husband died in a farming accident, Nellie called him when something broke. Sol had been in her house maybe five or six times in a couple of years, dealing with a water heater or a dishwasher seal or whatever. On all those occasions, there had been no more than fifteen or twenty words between them. Which perhaps why he was taken aback so by her statement. After centering himself, he said, "My wife isn't here, so why would I be wanting sex now?"

It was an attempt to take the moral high ground. And perhaps something of a volley against her serve. Besides, having been married less than a year, Sol never had a thought about anyone but Jan. Nellie replied, "You men are all that way. You do something nice for a woman and you have to have your reward."

Sol regarded her with some care, feeling a bit sad for her opinion of him. He really had only come to fix the door. It also suddenly occurred to him that they were not only fix-it-man and customer, but man and woman – no, *married* man and *unattached* woman – alone together in her house. Thinking back on it now, he could still feel that vulnerable knot in the pit of his stomach, and he remembered putting his tools back in the toolbox quicker than usual.

"Call me if you need anything else fixed. I'll send you a bill," he said over his shoulder as he moved to his father's rusty old truck, not wishing to give the awkwardness of the occasion any further opportunity. He told her to call, but he sincerely hoped she wouldn't.

On the way back to town, Sol had waxed philosophical. *Such is the lot of women in Monroe County,* he thought to himself. Painting a very specific incident with the broadest of strokes was what he often did when facing something uncomfortable. He saw in Nellie the general lack of education and opportunity afforded women in rural Wisconsin, and the prescribed roles into which the vast majority fell, like the little silver balls in one of those tilty puzzles. And it was so different from what Sol had learned at home.

Despite that empty chair, Sol had always been thankful for the way his dad treated his mother. It was their example that helped him to see manhood as more than being king of a proverbial castle. He had grown up knowing his mom

– and thus, *women* – as persons with opinions and skills and faults and worth just like anyone, male or female. As he grew older, he learned how unusual his family's household was by comparison to those of most of his friends.

It was the '50s, after all. Those over-glorified days when men were quite usually the breadwinners and women the bakers of the bread. "Keep 'em barefoot and in the kitchen," men were heard to say, only half-jokingly. Barbie dolls in the bedroom and Donna Reed everywhere else; that was the cultural norm in Monroe County.

But Sol's parents lived differently than that. On those occasions when Sol's father was home at the Severson dinner table, conversation could be heard – real dialogue with freedom to express opinions and to disagree. Del Severson was a strong union man, and a Democrat; his wife, Morgan Bakken Severson, was inclined a bit right leaning, politically. They each modified a bit toward the center over the years, but the point is that they modified one another. The lesson which deeply nurtured Sol and his sister Maura was about respect. Mutual respect. They didn't know it at the time, of course, but they had been given the gift of adulthood long before they were chronologically anywhere near it.

With the steam now filling the bathroom, Sol remembered the drive back to town after the Nellie incident, and the scenes of rural decline. Even back then, the signs were everywhere. Unpainted farmhouses – huge, boxy structures that were once home to large, productive farm families – now looking like mausoleums in a forgotten boneyard. Barns in varying states of disrepair, some with fallen roofs and nearly all with empty stanchions, littered the countryside like so many beggars shouting, "Will Work for Food!" But the passersby, with stereos blaring and eyes fixed on the empty road ahead, barely noticed.

Sol remembered once stopping along the road. He was high atop Macker Hill, from which you could see a good 20 miles or so in almost any direction. He counted all the barns, clustered as they were with mostly abandoned silos on once-busy family farms. "...*twenty-one, twenty-two, twenty-three*," he counted aloud. Twenty-three farms! Twenty-three family businesses, growing grain for silage and for sale, raising chickens for eggs and for butchering, and raising livestock for breeding and for meat and for milk. Twenty-three families, each with, say, three kids on average. That's sixty-nine kids and forty-six adults, all living and working and neighboring in this part of Monroe County. *Where are they now? Where did they all go?* He grew up a town kid, but it still made him feel depressed. Uncle George and Aunt Christine were among those farm families, and Sol's family times out on their farm were some of his better childhood memories.

He went to school with so many kids from Monroe County farm families. Of course, there was a sort of us and them thing – "the townies vs. the farm kids" – with the usual jockeying for social validity and bragging rights. But as they grew up together, Sol remembered feeling some measure of envy for the way those farm kids tended to approach life. Most kids had some responsibility at home, like taking out trash or mowing the lawn. But those farm kids had "chores." Every day there were chores to do, some before school even. Calves and pigs and chickens had to be fed; eggs had to be gathered; barns had to be cleaned; dairy cows required milking twice a day. Sol remembered the high school basketball and football coaches even made allowances in the practice schedule for kids who had to go home right after school to do chores on the family farm. He kind of looked up to those kids. He admired their sense of place and participation in the work and life of their families. There was a sort of rhythm to it all, like a kind of human machine, thrumming along.

As he finished his shower, Sol's mind drifted back once again to the experience with Nellie. It took years before he realized that *she* was the one wanting sex. It had never occurred to him at the time. But maybe making the offer into an accusation was her way of deflecting shame for wanting something beyond what she had. *It must be a hell of a thing to go through life feeling so ashamed*, he thought. He never did tell Jan about Nellie. Truth be told, he kind of liked the idea that another woman was willing to have sex with him. Sol kept that card hidden away in a secret place, so he could take it out and look at it every once in a while. It wasn't only the women of Monroe County who could be dissatisfied with their prescribed roles.

"Man! That trip to Tomah really dragged me into the past!" Sol said aloud as he surveyed himself in the bathroom mirror. He slapped his cheeks with both hands as he looked himself in the eye, "Snap out of it!" And with this rejoinder he finally left the misty memories of Tomah to rejoin the present, completing his morning transmogrification. When he emerged from the bedroom, dressed in an Armani suit, clean-shaven and scented with the air of self-assurance, Sol could have fooled anyone into believing he was a confident and secure member of the elite class. Never mind that he spent his late night in dreams about fish and fathers and childhood friends and fire, or that he spent his shower time daydreaming about long-past encounters with rural dissolution and farm kids.

---

The drive to work was the usual tedium. It was always the same: how to balance the need for acute attentiveness with the sheer, chronic monotony of the task. Being in the midst of thousands of people, all in large, rolling machines, many talking on cell phones or lost in the obnoxious banter of morning talk radio, and with the entire, tightly formed mass moving in three contiguous lanes at 70 miles per hour or more does not allow for much mental freedom. But Sol had developed the knack of allowing his mind to wander just enough.

Usually, his commuting thoughts roved among the tasks of the day and of the upcoming week. But this morning his awareness was filled by the memory of that awful dream. He tried to relive the experience, running it over and over in his mind, as if commanding its re-existence could contain its effect on him. The river and his father. The capsizing boat. The fish. The fire. And Tim. *I wonder what ever became of Tim?* he thought suddenly.

Sol hadn't thought about his boyhood friend for years. Even in youth, he hadn't felt particularly close to Tim. He'd been a convenient friend at the time, when most of the other boys Sol's age always seemed more readily clumped into group affiliations than either he or Tim was inclined to be. Neither of them was particularly athletic. Tim lacked the physical prowess, and Sol never acquired the competitive spirit. They were both misfits. Maybe that's why their boyhood friendship never lasted past high school.

Sol was glad to get to the office. Enough of the Tomah world. *Too much drama.* He was even glad to see Emma, so glad that he responded to her cheery greeting with a little pat on her shoulder. "My but aren't we in a fine mood this morning!" Emma said, ebullient as ever.

"Yes, we are," Sol replied, happy to have successfully contrived a fine mood. And soon he was reading his newspaper, drinking his coffee, going through his daily list of things to do and happily, intentionally, avoiding thoughts of the past several days.

# CHAPTER SIX

Amy took in the sweet, acrid smoke from the water pipe, trying hard not to choke and cough like a kid. She held the acrid smoke as deep in her lungs as she could, just like Jax taught her. Soon the familiar, warm sensation folded over her like a foamy blanket, stimulating and relaxing all at once. She lay back into Jax's chest and floated for a while.

Jax was a senior at Lancashire High School, and kind of a nerd. His scruffy, light brown hair sloughed around without much apparent direction, and that, along with his propensity for wearing old sweatshirts and baggy jeans, gave him the look of an unwashed artist. But Amy, only sixteen years old and a sophomore, was flattered when he'd first asked her out a couple of months earlier. She knew Jax was a loner, and that he got pushed around sometimes by some of the jocks. Maybe that's what drew her to him, in a way. She always had been a sucker for the underdog. Plus, he was a senior.

So, they started hanging out after school, and when he suggested getting high, she tried to respond like it was something she regularly did, not wanting to appear naive. After she coughed and turned several shades of red with her first toke, it was obvious she was a novice. But Jax was cool about it. He didn't make her feel stupid or self-conscious at all, which Amy found endearing. He helped her learn how it's done, and before long, she was hitting it like a pro. She grew to enjoy it, even if it did burn her lungs every time she first inhaled the smoke.

Amy felt Jax slipping his hands under her sweater, and she snuggled back against him. They hadn't gone "all the way," but she was beginning to think it was inevitable.

Almost all her friends had been having sex for some time. A lot of them had pretty much free reign at home with parents gone for one reason or another on a regular basis. It was pretty easy not to get caught.

Still, Amy held out, hoping for a sense of deep connection with someone first. She hadn't really found any such closeness with Jax, who basically wanted just to get high and fool around whenever they were together. He certainly wasn't long-term boyfriend material. But the combined sensation of the THC in her brain and his hands on her breasts felt good enough to be *some* sort of connection. And her body was certainly responding.

His right hand moved below her waist, and something inside Amy's mind said, "no."

She stood up and readjusted her clothing. "It's time for you to take me home now," she said.

Jax groaned. "Oh, come on, Amy! We've got something good here. I want you so bad! Don't wreck it!" He was whining.

All at once, Amy felt a well of contempt building up inside her. "Jax, take me home now or I'll start walking." Her commanding tone surprised even her.

He jumped up off the couch and blew past her to the front door. "Fine," he groused. "Come on."

All the way home not a word was spoken, and that was fine with Amy. She liked being desired, and having a senior taking her out was pretty good for her cred with all her friends, but she wasn't going to be groped and prodded all the time. *This can't be all there is*, she thought to herself. After dropping her off, Jax sped away without a good-bye.

Inside, Amy's mother was in the family room, reading. Just for a moment, Amy thought about telling her. It occurred to her that talking to her mom about this might feel really good. But she worried about the smell of the weed on her clothes. And when she heard her mom ask the usual question, her response was automatic: "Fine, and yours?" She didn't even wait for a response. "Cool. Well, I have homework." And up the stairs she went, as usual, enfolding herself in the sheltering arms of her bedroom. As she threw her books on the desk and flopped down on the bed, she suddenly felt more alone than she ever had. The tears flowed, but silently.

Jan, of course, had a sense something was wrong, but she never knew how to approach Amy. In fact, it wouldn't be too far off to call it fear. Back in the Twin Cities, Jan's own family had been all about propriety and duty. Jan's mother was a housewife and her father worked for the Hennepin County Clerk's office as a civil servant. To say her parents were emotionally distant would hardly touch the surface of the deep lake of silence in which Jan was raised. Consequently, as Jan approached the normally rebellious teen years, she never acted out. In fact, she never took any risks at all. She was the perfectly obedient daughter of Herb and Dorothy Larson, and she tried as best she could to make her parents proud of her.

Her brothers, on the other hand, took rebelling to a whole different level. Bobby was in and out of Juvenile Hall for a variety of offenses, and his younger brother, Jeff, did everything he could to outdo Bobby in obnoxiousness. Jan could recall the many trips to family counselors, trying to find a way to fix those bratty brothers of hers. Bobby and Jeff had both mellowed a bit with age, but neither of them had amounted to much. She hadn't seen Bobby in almost ten years, and Jeff used to call asking for help until Jan finally said no; he hadn't called since.

Needless to say, Jan's mother had provided little guidance and even less role modeling in dealing with a young girl approaching adulthood. While Jan wanted desperately to be close to Amy, she also wanted desperately not to do anything that might drive Amy away. The worst thing Jan could imagine was if Amy were to feel as distant from her as Jan had grown to feel toward her own mother. So, as she sat pondering what might be wrong and what she might do about it, Jan once again found herself retreating to her book.

---

This being a Thursday, Sol was spending his afternoon on the golf course with a number of colleagues and major clients. It was a practice of business he inherited from those who worked at Argenta for years before he got there; his participation was expected. He initially had to buy clubs and clothes for golfing, and he took a couple of months of lessons over his first winter at Argenta. Although he hadn't looked forward to it at all, Sol surprised himself by actually learning to enjoy the game. The time with the people, on the other hand, he merely tolerated. All the useless banter and false bravado, the claims of romantic conquest and complaints about marriage and children. It was more soap opera than Sol could tolerate sometimes, but he told himself, "You do what you have to do." And he consoled himself with the notion that at least he was getting some exercise.

When he got home that evening, he was glad to find Jan was out shopping and Amy was in her room as usual. He poured himself a scotch and sank into his easy chair, thankful for the solitary peace and quiet. After an hour Jan woke him and he went up to bed.

# CHAPTER SEVEN

Halloween was fast approaching, and Halloween was a big deal in Oakton Lakes. A trend of decreasing attendance at the Lancashire High Homecoming event had been noted over the past several years, and on investigation it came out that more recent alums had little interest in returning, and older alums were scattered all over, making attendance costly and often impossible for them. As a result, the high school decided to focus instead on a big Halloween Masked Ball, to which current students and their families were invited, as well as alums. They still had a homecoming football game, but it had become largely ceremonial, more to do with the schedules of the other schools in the conference than any need to keep in touch with alumni.

This was the third year of the Masked Ball, which had been growing in attendance each year. Jan, Amy, and Sol looked forward to the event. They scheduled a shopping trip three or four weeks in advance, when they'd all head into the city together to get new costumes and makeup. They would plan to meet at a scheduled time for lunch at an Applebee's near the mall, and this was the rule: each person shopped alone, and there was to be no peeking at costumes ahead of time. All had to wait until the night of the ball to reveal their respective characters.

When the day came for their trip, the Severson family all piled into Sol's car and headed out to the big party and costume store about 20 miles away in Elgin. Of all the days in the year, this day of shopping for Halloween costumes had become the most enjoyable. Sol wasn't initially thrilled with the idea, being one who prefers to keep to himself. But after seeing how excited Jan and Amy got over the whole thing, he overcame his normal social avoidance and kind of got into it. Somehow, the usual difficulties of work and struggling with various parent/child battles dissipated as they each headed off to search for whatever they needed to become someone else.

The inevitable progression of autumn was asserting itself more and more as they made the annual trip. Sol always looked forward not only to the "familyness" of the costume-buying trip but also to the fall colors that graced the journey. But something was different this year. Fall was being a bit stubborn and grumpy, offering only muted colors, and not much of those. And Mother Nature was not the only unenthusiastic party. Amy was unusually quiet, sitting in the back seat with her ear buds and her music, her nose buried in her phone.

"Amy, have you come up with some fun ideas for your costume?" Sol asked. No response. He adjusted the rearview mirror until she became visible. She was texting furiously, and then she let out an exasperated sigh, tossing her phone on the seat next to her as though it had insulted her. She began to stare out the window, the earbuds dangling like some barrier to the outside world. Sol's initial response was to dismiss her sullenness as typical teenage stuff. But there was a sadness in her eyes that alarmed him a bit.

"Amy!" Sol shouted this time, loud enough that Jan even startled.

"What?! Jesus! I'm just listening to some music. What do you want?"

"Nothing, really, I just wondered if you were okay."

Amy rolled her eyes and replaced her earbuds as she said, "Just want to listen to my music." Her gaze returned to the gray skies as she resumed her role of traveling incommunicado. Her phone chirped again, and she picked it up. Jax again. She tossed the phone down in disgust. As he watched her in the mirror, Sol's heart sank. *So much for "familyness."*

When they got to Elgin, they all went their separate ways, got their respective costumes, and met for their traditional Applebee's lunch, but it was as if some sentence had been handed down. All the way home nothing was said. No conversation at all. When Sol asked what was wrong, all he got was, "Nothing. I'm fine. Just leave me alone." He looked over at Jan, and she was extending the fingers of both hands, pressing in a downward motion which seemed to say, "Just back off. Don't overreact." Sol knew this was the right thing to do as a parent; inside he felt an empty longing that would not go away.

They got home and settled into bed, but Sol's emptiness amplified into a feeling of worthlessness. His mind drifted back to the image of that empty chair at the Severson dinner table when he was a boy. He grew up thinking that his father really liked being away from home and family, that being a husband and father was a burdensome chore which his work gave him license to avoid. Not so for Sol. He was truly devoted to Jan and Amy. He treasured his time at home with them. But right now, as he lay there for almost two hours, cocooned in his emptiness and unable to sleep, he imagined himself sitting in that dinner table chair, except it was here in his own home and with his own family, and no one noticed he was there. Although his daughter was just down the hall and Jan was lying right next to him, at that very moment Sol was feeling as alone as death itself.

# CHAPTER EIGHT

As October advanced against the dog days of summer, the preparations intensified for the Halloween Masked Ball at Lancashire High School. Posters were everywhere, and all the digital billboards were flashing invitations. Everyone seemed to be getting more and more excited. Everyone, that is, except for Amy.

In the couple of weeks since their family shopping trip, Amy's sullen and solitary presence in the Severson family only intensified. Every attempt to get her to open up, to say what was wrong, to break through her icy cold shell, was rebuffed. Sol was beginning to get worried. He even talked to Jan about visiting her former therapist for advice. But Jan said it was just a phase. "No need to catastrophize everything," she said, using a term she learned from her therapist. Sol knew she was right: he did tend to overreact sometimes.

But when the day of the ball arrived, Amy finally was the one who came to them. "Can't we just stay home this time?" she said. "I just don't feel like going. I know I've been a jerk the past couple of weeks, but I really want to stay home."

"Can you tell us why you don't want to go?" Jan said, moving toward her and gentling her hair.

"It's just something…" she trailed off, shaking.

"Amy, look at me?" Sol invited, and he lifted her chin a bit with his right hand. "What is it?" The tears burst forth like water from a failed dike as she pulled out her phone.

"I was seeing this guy, Jax. You remember?" She told her parents about him a while ago, but they hadn't heard anything about him for several weeks, at least. They never thought to bring it up, assuming it to be just another teen thing.

"Yes, I remember," Sol told her. "What about him?"

"I broke it off with him about six weeks ago. But he's been calling and texting. I kept ignoring him but look!" She showed them the text log, indicating over 250 texts she said were from Jax. "And there were a bunch of calls, too, until I blocked his number. When I see him at school, I head the other direction, but it seems like he's always there, staring at me with this weird look. I know he's going to be there tonight. And he even texted a couple of times that if I didn't talk to him, I was going to regret it."

"Let's sit down and talk about this," Sol said, and he guided Amy to the den. Jan's worried look was apparent as she put her arm over Amy's shoulders. "First off," Sol began, "how intense was this relationship? Did he ever have any reason to see you as a couple? Or is this just wishful thinking on his part?"

"We hung out a lot for a few weeks," Amy replied, "but it wasn't going anywhere. I got tired of him and just backed away. But he wouldn't quit. The more I told him it was over, the more he pushed. Finally, I even blocked him on my phone. But then he started following me. He even got a different phone with a new number. It's like he was some creepy stalker! And when he said I'd regret it if I didn't talk to him, I got scared."

While this was certainly disturbing news, Sol actually breathed a sigh of relief. *Finally! Finally, something to explain all this misery over the past couple of weeks.* "Listen," he told her, "this guy is certainly obsessed with you, but I can't imagine it will turn into anything dangerous. Still, how about if we let the security people know to keep a special eye out for you in case he starts bothering you at the Ball. Then we'll notify the school authorities on Monday so they can intervene. If it goes any further, we'll contact the police. But as for tonight, trust me: if this Jax dude tries to mess with my little girl, he's going to find some attention he doesn't want, and it's going to come from me!"

Amy wiped her eyes. "Are you sure? It's really going to be okay?"

Sol hugged her, pulling Jan in, too. "Nobody's going to mess with my little girl. Either one of them," he said, looking into Jan's worried eyes. He hoped she might be proud of him. *No need to catastrophize*, he could hear her saying. But that worried look never quite left her.

With the household tension finally relieved, each of them got their costumes on. After they all were ready, Sol did the countdown: "Three...Two...One...Okay!" And they each emerged. Jan had an absolutely great Hippie Chick outfit with a long, blonde, straight wig, looking every bit the Joni Mitchell of her youth. She had even dug out Sol's old guitar and had it strapped on her back. Amy was a truly scary vampiress, with fangs and bloody makeup around her mouth and a full-length cape with a high collar, and a tight-fitting (too tight-fitting, but Sol wasn't about to spoil the mood by complaining) black spandex one-piece body suit. As for Sol, he found a Col. Sanders outfit, complete with white suit, black Kentucky bow tie, a white wig and moustache-goatee, and fake wire-rim glasses. He stuffed a flattened accent pillow in his pants for a bigger belly.

They all laughed out loud at the sight of one another. As they got ready to head out the door, it seemed like all was back to normal.

# CHAPTER NINE

Jax Demuth woke with a start. It was early afternoon, and he still felt the remnants of last night's drugs. This was the day of the Halloween Masked Ball. He intended to make it a day to remember.

His bedsheets had found their way onto the floor of his bedroom along with most of the clothes he owned, some of which were still in folded piles from the last time his mother did his laundry. He shuffled off to the bathroom, and after relieving himself, stood before the mirror in his underwear. The thin, pale creature looking back at him belied the "true" man he knew himself to be. "Fuck you," he said to his mirror-image self. "Today, things are gonna change."

He fired up a doobie he got from his jacket pocket and lay back on his bed. "I need some music to get me in the mood," he said to himself. He found his old iPod and ran past a couple dozen songs, all grunge, for the most part, till he found his favorite: *Creep*, by Radiohead. He clicked it on, turned the volume on max, and lay back down as the music and the marijuana swirled to a great vortex of feeling and song. If anyone had even walked by the house, they could not have avoided hearing Jax shouting out the chorus: *But I'm a creep. I'm a weirdo. What the hell am I doing here? I don't belong here...*

His head filled up with thoughts of Amy, Jax lay there until he began to think about all the others. *All the cool people. Everybody who pushed me around. Everybody who kicked me to the curb.* "Amy... I thought you were special," he said out loud. If he had only let himself cry, all the rest of it might never have happened. But he wasn't going to let them win. Not today. Not ever again.

He shot up and sat down at the cluttered desk beside his bed and turned on his laptop. A sneering smile crawled across his lips as he began to type out what would be his famous creation. When he got it the way he wanted it, he saved it to the hard drive, and left the document open on his computer screen where someone would find it later. As he got up to get dressed, he surveyed his clothes from the day before, lying in their customary place on the floor alongside his bed. *No*, he thought to himself. *Not today. Today is not going to be an ordinary day. Today deserves something special.*

Searching through the piles of clean laundry and the drawers of his dresser, he found what he was looking for: black khakis, a solid black T-shirt, and a black hoodie. He even found black socks to wear inside his Gore-Tex boots, which were not black, but a very dark, mahogany brown. *Close enough.* After donning the special attire, Jackson David Demuth considered his image once more in the mirror on his dresser. "That's better," he said. But something was still lacking.

He headed downstairs to the kitchen, bypassing the breakfast his mother had laid out for him before she left for her job at the local hospital cafeteria. He went instead down to the basement, to what had been his father's workshop. Flipping on the 300-watt work light bulb, he saw what he was after. He opened the unlocked doors to his uncle's gun case and surveyed the contents: a Glock 17 9mm with ten clips and a speed loader; an expensive collector's edition IPSC twentieth anniversary Colt Tactical .45 automatic, worth a couple thousand dollars; a variety of .22 target shooting rifles and handguns; a classic Smith and Wesson snub-nose .38; and the big daddy: an AK-47 Kalashnikov assault rifle. He had inherited this impressive collection after his uncle Joe had died in what was first called a freak hunting accident. Shortly afterward, though, Jax's father, Donny Demuth, began serving a twenty-years to life sentence for killing his own brother. He was ten years in. And while Jax was only in third grade at the time and had no way to understand why his dad was taken away from him, over the years the fear Jax had of his dad's violent temper had morphed into a distant respect. He hated the man, but he also longed to be as tough and powerful as the man he imagined his father to be. And as he stood here now, proudly surveying his gun collection and virtually bursting with a syllogistic sense of power, Jax was viewing both his inheritance and his legacy.

He wanted to pick the assault rifle, because he loved the feel and look of the gun and of himself holding it. But the weapon was too large to easily conceal. He opted instead for the Glock. He placed it into his knapsack along with the speed loader and all the clips, and after some consideration, he also grabbed the .45 and a full clip of ammo and threw it in as well. He zipped up the bag. The sun was going down. Time to get ready.

# CHAPTER TEN

The campus of Lancashire High School sat on nearly 70 acres, 40 of which had been highly fertile and productive farmland. The school was sort of a flagship of modern suburban excess. No expense was spared in the planning or in the realization of the LHS campus, as the busy and successful ex-urbanites supplanted scant resources of family time with rich investments in what they virtuously referred to as "our children's future." Despite being relative newcomers to the generally agrarian environs of Oak County, the money spent by all those who chose to live "in the country" was certainly needed. And after the more traditional inhabitants raised objections about building such a lavish school and the loss of so much rich farmland, some well-heeled ad exec coined a couple of slick phrases, like "this farmland will grow our children" and "turning plowshares into education" and "our children's future rising from the earth." In the weeks leading up to the bond referendum vote, those phrases were seen on yard placards and billboards and television ads throughout the area. As usual, the money won.

It had taken nearly two years to complete the building project, due in part to some weather-related delays, and in larger part to cost overruns, which required some skillful budget and appropriation "adjustments." Quite a few palms had gotten greased in the process, and there were rumors of various shady dealings and unscrupulous tactics; the usual fare served at the banquets of wealthy contenders for attention and positions of advantage. But finally, the school building was ready for use, and the grand opening was held. That was eight years ago.

On this night outside the school, the temperature was becoming a bit brisk, but it was a beautiful late autumn evening. The sun was beginning to settle back into nighttime's comfy pillow, enfolded by the sheets and blankets of the high, thin, western clouds which appeared in an astounding variety of deep umber and purple hues, brightest in a narrowing center and streaking into darkening edges to the north and to the south. Members of the Masked Ball committee were lighting the hundreds of sand candles that outlined the walkways and entryways to the gymnasium where the fest was always held. Each candle had been purchased for a $10 donation to the LHS Boosters, a committee formed to help fund sports and other extracurricular activities. It was not unusual for this event to raise $3,000 or more. Cars pulled into the parking lots with steadily increasing frequency, and the local sheriff's deputies assigned to provide security arrived, which occasion was duly noted by certain occupants of some cars, who were engaging in various forms of preparatory imbibing.

The Severson family needed no such augmentation to their evening. Having arrived with a newly relaxed family élan, the three masked characters chatted excitedly in anticipation. They arrived a bit earlier than usual, but Amy jumped out of the car, and with a "see you later," she headed off to find her friends. Having noticed a member of the security detail near the entrance, Sol also opened his door. Jan said, "I don't want to go in this early." Sol replied, "We won't. I'll be right back." He walked over to the deputy and shook his hand, introducing himself. He pointed out Amy as she was entering the building.

"That's my daughter, Amy. She's been getting some

pretty weird texts and phone calls from a kid who seems obsessed with her. She broke it off with him a few weeks ago, and he's made her feel pretty scared."

"Did he threaten her in any way?"

"He specifically referred to this night, but other than that, no."

"What's his name?"

"Jackson Demuth. He calls himself Jax. I only met the kid once. Not particularly impressed."

"I'll pass this on to the other officers, and we'll keep an eye out for anyone messing with Amy. I'm sure it'll be okay. These teenage love crises can seem more serious than they are."

"Yeah, I know. Still, I appreciate you looking out for my kid. Thanks." Sol shook the man's hand again and headed back to his car, where he found Jan adjusting her wig and her makeup.

"Did you call out the Secret Service?" she said, feigning a lack of concern, which he knew to be a façade.

"Yep. He's gonna pass the word, and they'll be on the lookout for all nefarious characters. You know, it's such a relief to know what was going on with her. Why can't she just tell us what's bothering her?"

"I don't know. I never could tell my mom anything, either. Part of the plan, I guess. At least she finally did speak up. Maybe we..." (she accented the "we" while making Sol look her in the eye) "...need to keep remembering that she did come to us. It was just that she came to us on her own timing, and not as soon as we wanted her to. Maybe we..." (there was that accent again) "...need to have a bit more patience and get less easily flustered."

Jan gave Sol a sly, loving smile, the sort of look that had

always charmed him. She was right, of course; he did tend to get easily worried. To "catastrophize," as she put it. She pulled him over for a quick kiss, which he made into more than that. "Hey, they're gonna think we're making out like a couple of kids!" she protested, though not very strongly. His eyes followed her fingers to the spot where they played with the fabric of her tie-dyed T-shirt above her breasts. She moved her hand under his chin, lifting his gaze back to her widening eyes. "Besides," she said, "you'll mess up my makeup and we might have to stay out here all night," coyly biting her lower lip in an incredibly sexy smile. "Come on! We're here early, so let's go in!" she said, suddenly opening the car door.

She got the guitar out of the back seat, and Sol stuffed his pillow-belly in place, and off they went, the corpulent Kentucky Colonel and the cool Canadian folk singer, arm in arm. *This is going to be a hell of a night*, Sol thought.

———————

Jax Demuth had also arrived early. With his backpack dangling off his left hand, he had walked right in through the darkened dance hall, right past all the excitement of preparations and busy, last-minute details being attended to by the LHS elite. Nobody noticed him. He knew they wouldn't. In fact, he'd counted on it. He found his way to a stall in the men's bathroom and pulled out the little sign he had printed out especially for this occasion: "CLOSED FOR REPAIRS." He taped the sign to the door of the stall, closed and locked the door behind him, sat down and waited.

# PART TWO: WINTER

Our destiny often looks like a fruit-tree in winter.
Who would think from its pitiable aspect that those rigid
boughs, those rough twigs could next spring again be green,
bloom, and even bear fruit?

Yet we hope it, we know it.

Johann Wolfgang Goethe, *Wilhelm Meister's Travels*, translated
from German by A.H. Gunlogson, from the later and enlarged edition
(1888)

# CHAPTER ELEVEN

Sol was sitting in the family room at home. The sun had somehow escaped his notice, and he was surprised to find himself sitting in the dark. Perhaps he had slept; he didn't recall. The bottle of Glen Morangie on the coffee table was almost empty, and the remote to the TV was in his lap, waiting – like Sol, maybe – to be put to use.

Earlier that day, Sol had finally found the gumption – for the umpteenth time – to once again start sorting through all the papers, the big and little scraps of what used to be his life. Over a year had gone by now since that awful night when everything unwanted took over. Terror, shock, loss, and sensational fame –all these became Sol's reality. These things outside of him snatched control, and he had neither the will nor the emotional strength to resist them. But as he sat at the desk – Jan's desk – every single word on each and every note or bill or memo – and especially the sympathy cards – struck him right through with an agonizing emptiness. Before long, he had retreated to his scotch. Again.

The fame was perhaps the worst of it for Sol, introvert that he was. Within a day of the tragedy, Oakton Lakes was swarming with TV broadcasting vans and reporters from every goddamned rag in existence – buzzards all – clamoring for some piece of saturnine carrion they could tear off and feed to their gossip-hungry consumers. The reporters took no time at all in learning of the killer's last message, left on the computer screen in his bedroom, which contained only three lines in centered, 72-point block letters: **FUCK YOU ALL**. All the news outlets depicted the message (with the first U blurred out, as if that made it more appropriate). The story was a feature item for over a week before other tidbits of titillating capacity replaced it. But even though the story fell off the news shelf of the major outlets, it was a couple of months before Sol's neighborhood was truly quiet again, and weeks more before he would dare venture out into his own yard. It's terrible to grieve. It's torture to grieve in a fishbowl.

The ravenous newshounds fixed on the Severson home because they had no place else to go. Sol sometimes watched those true crime shows that recounted the gory details of various serial murders and such. He knew that often in mass shootings there are numerous places to find a story. There is the finding of the killer, followed by an arrest and arraignment. There is the microscopic examination of the perpetrator's family, pored over like agar in a Petri dish. Then of course there is the lengthy trial and the eventual verdict. All these avenues provide fertile sources for facts or innuendos to publish and broadcast.

But in this case, and unfortunately for the news cycle, there had been no need for a trial. After killing Amy and Jan and twenty-six others, and after wounding sixty more, Jax's final victim was himself. Sol saw it all. The bullets ripping through "his girls," the ones he had promised to protect. The bullets tearing through so many others all around the gym.

And that last bullet... The memory played over and over in Sol's mind as if on a video clip: Jax is standing there like Nero, surveying his destruction and rapt with his own criminal power. He drops the Glock and replaces it with a .45 automatic, which he aims up under his chin. He has such a look of satisfaction on his face! Almost smiling, he looks as though he has just accomplished some major life event, like he's posing for his admiring onlookers. Sol couldn't get that horrible moment and that stupid kid's face – that awful, sardonic look – out of his mind. It haunted him even now.

It had all happened so quickly, no one was able even to react. Sol himself was not so much as grazed, and he could not for the life of him make sense of that fact. He never ducked for cover. He never really had time. Amy and Jan were the first two hit by the spray of ammunition, and Sol was standing right there with them. His arms cradled them, instinctively shielding them from bullets that could no longer harm them as they slumped to the floor. They died instantly. *Why them and not me?* Every time he thought of it, he ached to be with them, and he thought of it most of his waking hours, every day. Every single day.

There had been a lot of days since that October night. After the initial whirlwind of notifications and funeral preparations came the inevitable calls and offers of "if there's anything we can do." People apparently realize the impotence of such offers, because their frequency is indirectly proportional to the passage of time. One by one, the helpless, sincerely concerned friends faded away, till all that was left were those with no intention of helping, but hoping instead to snap a gut-wrenching photo, something to illustrate the pithy, maudlin verbiage ridiculously called a "human interest story." And after the passage of enough days, even those nosy newshounds finally moved on to unbury other bones.

Sol went back to work about a month after the funeral, but neither his heart nor his head was in it. On more than one occasion he found himself sitting in his office, newspaper in front of him, filled coffee cup cold and untouched, while he variously stared out the window or at the blank wall across from his desk. Four months went by, with the company tolerating Sol's lackluster performance. Argenta was a major corporate accounting and investment firm with over 700 employees, a number that could provide significant cover for the occasional underperforming worker.

But Sol began forgetting appointments, even with Emma's helpful reminders, to the point that a complaint or two found their way up the food chain to Henry Melisson, Sol's boss. When Emma buzzed him and said Mr. Melisson wanted to see him, Sol was not at all surprised. What was surprising was the compassion and understanding with which he was met by his boss. After expressing a sincere concern for Sol and sadness about what he had suffered, Melisson suggested that Sol take a six-month leave of absence, and the company would cover his salary for four of those months. Sol could use accumulated personal and vacation time, if necessary, to cover the remaining two months. And if along the way he felt ready to return earlier, he was welcome to do so. After shedding some mutual tears, the meeting ended, and Sol went home.

And so, began the mystery...

# CHAPTER TWELVE

The days turned into weeks, running together and flying like the late-autumn leaves which again were shining their death-colors in a gorgeous, restive display of foreboding. The first snows had already dusted the land, and an early chill frosted the roofs of the resplendent Oakton Lakes homes.

Sol rarely left the house. He stopped the newspaper; it had become embarrassing to see all the uncollected papers littering his driveway. Initially, he tried to resume the usual routine of sitting at the table with coffee and the local paper, but he found every word, irrespective of the story content, amounted to the same understanding: Jan and Amy were gone.

Sol would wander from room to room, from the front yard through the garage to the backyard. He would sometimes sit in one spot for hours, unmoving, not particularly bored, but totally unmotivated to go anywhere or do anything. He was not hungry much of the time. When he got hungry, he would call to have food delivered. And then, as often as not, when the food arrived, he would pay for it, set it on a table somewhere, and completely forget about eating it.

Nobody called. Except canvassers for some political campaign or the March of Dimes or someone offering to sell replacement windows. But many days went by with no contact at all. Sol began to feel himself slowly spiraling, moving downward, steadily downward, until he no longer noticed even what day it was, or what hour, or whether it was day or night. A cloud first shadowed him, then enfolded him, and eventually Sol began to take comfort in its existence.

---

He didn't remember having fallen asleep, but on awakening, Sol knew something was very wrong. Or perhaps just very unfamiliar. He lay there on his bed, uncovered as usual, his eyes moving back and forth across the ceiling, when suddenly he found himself nearer and nearer to it. To the ceiling! Was he floating? Yes! *I must be dreaming*, he thought, in words he heard as if someone else spoke them. Suspended there, lighter than himself, he began to find his bearings, such as they were, and soon he was able to move about with absolutely no effort at all, but merely by the propulsion of his thoughts. *Bathroom.* And in an instant, there he was by the bathroom door. Not that he cared, because even though he had just awakened from a long sleep, he apparently had no further need for that particular room. Apparently, it was with his internal functions as with his body itself: he merely had to think it so, and it was so. Such an utterly fantastic state! Sol began to revel in this newfound freedom, as though all the former weight of grief and sadness and loneliness and emptiness had been cast off.

As Sol acclimated himself to his strange, new world, he began to move about the house. First, the family room. There was Jan's desk, full of papers and mess just as he remembered. But gone was the previously attendant heartache associated with it. The desk no longer seemed attached to Jan or him or to anyone. It was simply a desk. As he looked around the room, Sol happened to see outside that it was dark. He looked for a clock but found none. Somehow, the clock on the wall – the one he and Jan had received from her law firm for their fifth anniversary – was simply not there. And something else: although it was dark outside, here in the family room there was plenty of light, even though no lamps were lit. *This is weird*, he said to himself. And again, the words had sound as though spoken. His ears heard the words; his lips had not created them. He only thought, "This is weird," and the words *happened*.

Sol moved on to the kitchen, which was in disarray. Jan would never have tolerated it this way, and neither would he before... And instantly the memory of Jan and Amy and what happened came rushing back like a violent straight wind. He sank down inside something he could not identify. It was as though he were inside one of those cars in a wind tunnel, with colored smoke streamers flailing away. He saw visions of Jan and Amy rushing toward and by and past him, yet inside he was untouched. Inside, all was calm and quiet. He could see the images – some pleasant or even hilarious, some ugly and deathly – but each one, like Phaeton's chariot, rushed by and around him, a filigree of fragments.

It suddenly occurred to Sol that he needn't remain here in this... whatever this was, and he *thoughted* himself out to the garage. There was his Honda, looking frightfully unkempt and filthy, even if it was in its perfect, tennis-ball-guided spot. Sol had always been rather persnickety about keeping his car clean, but somehow the dirt and grime just didn't matter to him. He noticed the empty spot Jan's Prius used to occupy. The garage door was, of course, closed. He thought of opening it to wander out to the yard, but the door didn't move. *Hmmm,* he heard himself *thinksay*. He tried again, focusing his thoughts on the garage door, willing it to open, but it did not. *But I want to go outside!*

he thinksaid, and immediately he found himself in the front yard. Apparently, his newfound ability to mobilize objects with his thoughts was limited to only himself. *So, no telekinesis? No spoon-bending tricks?* he thoughtsaid.

He looked around the yard and the neighborhood, and all seemed defiantly typical. He wandered out toward the street and a couple of people passed by, one walking a dog, another jogging, but neither of them took notice of Sol, not even to intentionally avoid interaction. They seemed to truly not see him at all. *Am I, perhaps...* the word sort of stuck in the back of his throat, but he couldn't avoid it: *Am I dead? If I am dead, where are Jan and Amy?* He began to cast his vision every which way, hoping to discern some sign that could lead him to his girls.

But the neighborhood murmured normalcy. The perfect, manicured lawns still protruded like green tongues thrust outward from the pursed lips of the brick-front façades. *What is this?* he thinksaid. *What is happening? What am I? Who am I??*

A momentary sense of wonderment engulfed him, as the strangeness of this new existence began to assert itself on his consciousness. *I can't open the garage door, but I can be anywhere I want? Instantly?* The possibilities began to burst forth like energy from a splitting atom: *Anywhere? Really? I can be anywhere?*

Sol went back into the house, and maybe he slept. Then (he had no idea how much time had gone by) he heard something. Some pounding, followed by a voice, calling out, and then glass breaking. He remembered feeling a twisted knot of fear in his belly, and then he saw the gun. That's when he sat back down in the "tunnel." For some reason, he felt very safe there. And just as before, glimpses of people began to flash by. Jan and Amy, and Maura, but when she was little. And his mother, back when Sol was a boy. *These are just memories*, Sol thinksaid. But they seemed more than mere memories. As he sat there, safe in his wind tunnel place, the entire scene began to revolve and change. Darkness interrupted by bright lights, images of strange beings he could not make out, shadows menacing, speaking unintelligibly. He supposed he must be dreaming, or maybe even dreaming about dreaming. He closed his eyes against the invading threat, and tried to think about Jan.

# CHAPTER THIRTEEN

"And last, but not least, we had a new admit to room 614, a Mr. Delbert Severson. His vitals are stable; in fact, just about as stable as things get. He appears to be quite catatonic." It was 3:45 p.m., and the charge nurse, Anna Gable, was giving report to the oncoming second-shift crew on E-Ward, the nickname given to the sixth floor East Wing of St. Joseph's Medical Center devoted to psychiatric inpatient care. "Mr. Severson was brought in this morning about 10:30. He had not apparently eaten or drunk anything for days, and his clothes were saturated with urine and fecal matter. He was severely dehydrated and his 'lytes were depleted, but we started him on IV fluids and he is responding. He's lucky a coworker happened to check on him; I don't think he would have made it much longer."

"Any family?" Angela Corrales spoke up.

"Not anyone close. You remember the Lancaster High shootings?" A collective gasp and a hushed series of murmurs briefly sucked the air out of the room as those who had been working at St. Joseph's a year ago remembered the various ways she or he had been impacted by that carnage.

"You don't mean he's Jan Severson's husband?" Angela looked startled.

"'Fraid so." Anna looked up after Angela spoke. "Angie, did you know Jan?"

"Yeah. I mean, not real well, but she mentored me on my orthopedic rotation my senior year of nursing school. So tragic. Her and her daughter both."

"And now her husband," Anna added. "Senseless massacre. The gift that just keeps on giving."

"But I don't remember the name 'Delbert.' I thought she called him by some other name," Angie said. "Something shorter."

"Well, maybe when he decides to rejoin the world, he can tell us what he likes to be called. For now, he needs basic nursing care. Monitor fluids, eye and mouth care, toileting; you know the drill. Dr. Singh has not ordered an NG tube yet, but if we can't get some calories on board pretty quick, that will be next. So, who wants to work with Mr. Severson tonight?"

"I will," Angie said. "I'll see if I can get him to eat a little something. Maybe some Ensure, at least."

"And not that any of us don't know," Anna said, "but it's good to review how catatonia presents. We don't see many full-blown cases here, so just remember not to push. Gentle voice, speak the patient's name on every approach, ask permission for every necessary touch but don't expect a response. And remember also: sometimes these patients come out with a bang. You never know what might trigger a catatonic patient to 'wake up,' but they have been known to do so quite violently, so keep aware of your surroundings."

With the report finished, all moved out to the floor to engage their respective patients. Angie felt a very strong need, for some reason, to head directly for Sol. When she got to his room, Sol was sitting in a straight-backed chair beside his hospital bed. He wore pajamas which the deputy sheriff had been kind enough to dig out of Sol's dresser. The pajamas looked about three sizes too big on him, since he had lost almost forty pounds in recent weeks. As Angie approached him for the first time, the impression she had was of a ten-year-old boy wearing his father's nightclothes.

"Mr. Severson? I'm Angela Corrales. You can call me Angie. I'm a nurse here at St. Joseph's hospital, and I will be your nurse this evening." There was no noticeable response. "Mr. Severson, I need to take your blood pressure and pulse, okay?" Again, no response. Angie raised Sol's arm a bit to allow space for the BP cuff. His arm stayed outward, suspended awkwardly. *Just like in the textbooks*, Angie thought to herself. She pumped up the sphygmomanometer and listened for the pulses – 160 over 85. *Pretty high for a thin, sedate man*, she thought. She took his pulse, which was 78. Again, quite elevated for a person sitting in a chair. *There must be a lot going on inside this man*, Angie mused. She removed the cuff and moved Sol's arm back to a resting position. She moved to face Sol, looking directly into his eyes (which registered nothing). "You're doing just fine, Mr. Severson. I look forward to spending some time with you this evening. I'll be back soon." And with that, Angela Corrales moved on to her next patient.

# CHAPTER FOURTEEN

As Emma Prentiss drove to work on this particular Thursday, it took some effort to keep her mind focused on the driving. It was she who had called to check on Sol, and after getting no answer three days running, it was she who had phoned the Oak County sheriff's office to request a wellness check, an action which no doubt saved Sol's life. That was yesterday morning. And when the deputy sheriff phoned back that afternoon to inform her of Sol's situation, she hadn't been at all surprised; something inside her just knew Sol was in trouble.

Emma had worked as Sol's secretary for almost seven years, and while their relationship had always been fairly formal and hierarchic (she continued to call him "Mr. Severson"), she had been with him long enough to have learned a bit about the man who lived under the boss's veneer. He was not an easy man to know, at least not by Emma's definition. Sol was very private, sharing very little of a personal nature. Emma, on the other hand, was an open book, ready to engage in conversation with just about anyone on just about any topic, and willing to offer up information about herself, her friends, her hobbies, her beliefs, and especially her family, whom she referred to as "my life." It was, perhaps, the strength of those relationships in her close circle of family and friends that had nurtured a strong intuitive ability in Emma, an ability which enabled her to see past and through the barriers some folks build around themselves. People like Sol, for example.

For instance, there was the time when Sol and Jan were quarreling. Emma didn't have a clue what the fight was about, but she had connected the call from Jan, and she could tell that the discussion was heated. It was plain to see that when Sol left for lunch, he was disturbed. So, while Sol was at lunch, Emma went into his office and found the *Sun Times*, which was on his desk as usual. She thumbed through the pages until she found a large ad from a florist with big, beautiful roses on sale. She folded the paper so that the ad was right on top and placed the paper on the desk directly in front of Sol's office chair. After lunch, she was pleased when Sol buzzed her and asked her to order a dozen roses and have them sent to Jan at work. There was never a word spoken between them about it, but Emma believed Sol knew the hint was from her, and that he appreciated it.

But now Sol's office was empty, awaiting his return. Emma had been reassigned to assist various other account reps, but she was able to stay in her customary spot outside Sol's office. And this morning, having made her way once again to Argenta and to her desk, Emma's "life" was there to greet her. She always started her day with the smiling faces of her family. Even on those days when the commute was horrendous, when she got to her desk, it was those photos – not the pictures themselves, but the *actuality* of their subjects – which calmed and centered her. She was thirty-seven years old, and the only one of her siblings (she was the second of three girls) who had not yet married, but she was very involved in the lives of her sisters and their families. She loved her nieces and nephews as though they were her own, and everyone in the family knew it. It was much the same with her closest friends, too. And around her desk, the reminders of all those people to whom Emma was connected – by kinship or by friendship – surrounded her like a soft, warm quilt.

As she prepared to sit down and get to work, she glanced over at Mr. Severson's office through the glass wall that separated her desk from his. A tear trickled down her cheek. Something about the emptiness of that office and her awareness of her boss having been found so desperately alone made her extremely sad. Emma's heart was a big place, filled with her family, but there was plenty of room there for others, too. She made a plan right then and there to stop and see him after work, and then she turned her attention to the tasks of the day.

———————

Emma got permission to leave thirty minutes early, and as she headed toward her car, she began to feel an uncharacteristic bit of unease. She had always been drawn to helping someone in trouble, but for some reason the prospect of seeing Sol felt more urgent than usual. As she made the twenty-minute drive to St. Joseph's, she tried to imagine how Sol would look. She had only ever seen him in a business suit. How would he react to her seeing him as a patient on a mental ward? *What should I say to him?* she wondered.

Emma pulled into the visitors' parking area and found the information desk just inside the hospital's main entrance. "I'm here to see Mr. Severson," her usual reference came out automatically.

"First name?" came the inquiry from the kindly older woman in the pinkish volunteer frock.

"Mr. Delbert Severson," she clarified. The lady searched her computer screen. "I don't see a Delbert Severson," she replied. "Could he have been dismissed?"

"No, no way," she said, "he just came in yesterday afternoon. He's on the psychiatric floor."

"Oh, well patients on E-Ward don't show up on my patient list. I'm afraid I don't know if he's here or not. You can go up to the sixth floor and talk to the receptionist there. They may be able to help you."

Emma found the elevator and got off at the sixth floor. She followed the sign to the East Wing and approached the desk outside the locked, double door. A handsome young man occupying the desk looked up. "May I help you?"

"I would like to visit Mr. Delbert Severson," Emma said.

"Are you family?" the man asked.

"I am his secretary," Emma replied. "I'm the person who called the sheriff's office to check on him, and they called me back to tell me they brought him here."

"I'm sorry, but I can neither confirm nor deny that Mr. Severson is a patient here without the patient's consent. Do you know whether he signed consent for you to visit?" The young man's response sounded suddenly canned and legalistic.

"I rather doubt it," Emma said, sadly. "The deputy told me that he was totally unresponsive. He used the word 'catatonic.'" Emma's face fell as she imagined just what that word might mean in real life for Mr. Severson. The receptionist could see Emma's disappointment and the obvious concern on her face.

"I know this is very frustrating, but without that signed consent, I'm afraid there's nothing I can do. If you want to leave your name and contact information, I can forward it to the charge nurse, and if Mr. Severson is a patient here, she can attempt to obtain his permission for you to visit."

Emma wrote down her name and contact numbers at

home and at work, and as she turned to leave, her concern began to turn to irritation. *I'm the one who probably saved his life, and I know he's here, but they won't even let me see him! How can it help to cut someone off from people who care about him?*

# CHAPTER FIFTEEN

All at once Sol was sure he was awake, except that he found himself in some place he did not recognize. It was like a time he remembered when he was a kid back in Tomah. He had gone to see a Saturday matinee, and during the movie the town became engulfed in the thickest fog he had ever seen. When he emerged from the movie theatre, the sun was gone, and the fog was so overwhelming and intrusive that nothing was familiar. None of the usual landmarks were discernible. He remembered thinking that the fog seemed way too close, almost like it was breathing, and that it unnerved him. He was forced to walk his bike back home, counting the blocks to help him get his bearings. But now, here in this strange place, there were no blocks to count. All was odd, surreal even, and he had that same unsettled feeling as he did all those years ago in that mysterious fog.

A bright shadow approached him, holding something. A gun? There was a sharp pain in his arm, and suddenly he found himself seated again, secured in his wind tunnel. He began to anticipate the flashing images, and sure enough, there they were. *Am I just thinking these things or are they really there?* he thinksaid. Regardless, the images again flashed by, multi-colored and comet tailed. As he watched, they began to whirl and turn around him like a carnival ride with bright, colored lights and a streaming, cloudlike mist that sparkled like diamond dust.

The vision was mesmerizing, but the swirling motion was beginning to make him feel a little sick. He began to recall how he could maneuver with his thoughts, so Sol thinksaid, *Okay, time to slow down the show.* And almost

"Mr. Severson, do you remember me? My name is Angie, and I am your nurse this evening. You are at St. Joseph's Medical Center, and you are doing fine." She pulled up another chair and seated herself in front of Sol, placing herself between him and the window. "Mr. Severson, you have not had anything to eat for quite a while. The doctor is getting worried about your health if you don't take some food. I want it to be your choice, but if you don't decide to accept some food pretty soon, the doctor might order tube feeding, and that's not at all pleasant. You don't have to say anything right now, and you don't have to decide this instant, but I wanted to let you know."

Sol offered no indication he had heard or understood what Angie said to him. "Well," she continued, "I'll just sit here with you for a little while. Sometimes it's nice to just have some company." And with that, she pulled her chair over beside his and sat down. Not another word was spoken. After fifteen minutes had passed, Angie rose from her chair. "I have to go look in on my other patients now, Mr. Severson. I enjoyed sitting with you. I'll come back soon to look in on you."

She repeated this approach several times that evening, introducing herself and reminding Sol where he was, and encouraging him to consider eating something. She sat with him for ten or fifteen minutes each time, looking for any signs of receptivity or attempts by her patient to communicate. And then she would leave.

———

Sol was still on the merry-go-round, captivated by the sights and sounds that surrounded him: brightly colored and flashing images zipping by like fireflies, and dull, tonal bell sounds like from the barge ships on the river. He thought he smelled popcorn, and it made him aware of an ache in his stomach. He thought about the amazing conversation with little Maura, but something told him this was not actually happening – the merry-go-round, the colors and images flashing around him – none of it. Still, he was so enjoying this feeling of peace and safety that he was willing to go along for the ride a little longer.

He felt a hand on his shoulder and turned to see his Uncle George, looking much as Sol remembered him from those family times on the farm. George reached out his hand, and Sol grasped it in a heartfelt handshake. *I don't understand how this is happening, but it's very good to see you, Uncle George*, he thinksaid.

"It's good to see you, too, Sol. We sure had our good times when everybody came out to the farm, didn't we?"

*We sure did*, Sol thinksaid. *Those are some of my best memories.*

"Are they?" George looked right into Sol's eyes. "Good. Remember them. Make good use of them." And then Uncle George evaporated into the mist, just like little Maura had done.

---

When Angie came back around the 9:00 hour, she noticed that Sol's right hand was in a slightly different position than it had been. So, taking a chance, she went to the kitchen and brought back a plastic container of Ensure. She opened it, placed a straw inside, and closed Sol's hand around the bottle. "I want you to try to drink this, Mr. Severson. There's a straw in the bottle. It's good for you and it tastes good, too. It's time you ate something. You don't want that tube down your nose." As she went off to her next patient, she thought her tone may have sounded a bit menacing. *But if it gets through to him...* She really didn't relish the idea of inserting that NG tube.

———————

Sol got up and stepped off the merry-go-round, and he began to look around this strange place. The smell of popcorn was really punching a hole in his stomach, and it was getting harder and harder to ignore it. And he was thirsty, too. He thought he heard a voice just then, a gentle voice. Maybe a woman's voice? Jan? Could Jan have been trying to talk to him? Or maybe his mother? Sort of sounded like that "get to the table" voice. He sat quietly and tried to listen for that voice again, but it was gone. He thought maybe he'd wander around, look for a vendor. When he looked down, he found something in his hand. Some sort of drink with a straw had found its way into Sol's hand, so he tried it. It was smooth and creamy, like strawberry milk, which had been his favorite treat when he was a kid. Every day after school he would run into the kitchen and his mom would make strawberry milk for him. Even after he got old enough to make it for himself, she still made it for him. And although he never would admit it, Sol kind of enjoyed keeping that one little piece of his rapidly receding boyhood untouched. It was nice being taken care of by his mom. While he had no idea where the drink in his hand had come from, he was so hungry and thirsty that he drained it in no time.

———————

Angela Corrales was happy to report to her charge nurse at the end of her shift that Mr. Severson had consumed a bottle of Ensure. "He hasn't yet spoken or moved out of his chair, but I think the Prolixin and Elavil must be working. It's kind of amazing how quickly those drugs can kick in. He was only admitted yesterday morning, and it might be wishful thinking, but I maybe saw a little bit of awareness creeping in near the end of the shift, a bit of eye contact. And he did drink the Ensure, so I guess there's reason to be optimistic."

When Angie left that evening, she had to resist the urge to look in one more time on Sol, but she was scheduled to come back tomorrow morning, so she decided to wait. She wasn't sure what it was about him that drew her in. Maybe it was her connection to his wife, or maybe her compassion for the tragic loss he had suffered. But for whatever reason, when Angie got into her bed that night, her last thoughts were ones of anticipation. She was really looking forward to going to work tomorrow.

―――――――――

Morning snuck in under the cover of darkness the next day. It was winter, after all, and daylight was stingy and reticent this time of year. Angie arrived at work around 6:30, a bit earlier than usual. After hearing the report from the night shift, she again agreed to work with Sol, and just as she had yesterday, she looked in on him right away. Medications were being distributed and the nurse was about to give Sol his morning meds, so Angie decided to come back later.

The bright shadow approached him again, and Sol started to recoil. Was that a gun? No, it was a needle. A sharp pain in his arm again. Somebody injected him with something. *So that's what that was*, Sol thinksaid. He began to understand now, little by little, that this place he was in must be a hospital. Things were coming into better focus, and he was beginning to feel a little less scared. The truth was that the powerful medicines he had been receiving in those injections (coupled with his normalizing electrolytes) were having the desired effect. The fog of psychotic dreaming was slowly lifting.

Angie checked on Sol frequently throughout the day, and toward the end of her shift she found Sol seated in his same wooden chair, but in a noticeably more relaxed manner. The rigidity was gone, and she could see him moving his limbs a bit, readjusting his position. Remembering the unit director's cautioning, Angie approached Sol from the side, announcing herself well in advance in order to avoid startling him. "Mr. Severson?" she said. "I don't know if you will remember, but my name is–"

"Angie," Sol finished her sentence.

Angie was surprised and pleased to hear Sol's voice. "That's right!" she replied, with a smile. "I didn't know if you would remember me. Do you prefer to be called Delbert? Or maybe Del?"

A flood of associations spilled over in Sol's mind, recollections of his father and his grandfather, and of times he was picked on by the other kids chanting, "Del-Bert! Del-Bert!" He became lost in his memories for a bit. "Mr. Severson?" Angie gently intruded.

"I've always hated my first name. Since I was a kid, I've always been called 'Sol.' My middle name is Solomon, and people call me Sol. The words came out, but they felt thick, like speaking through a bowl of Jell-O.

"Well, Sol, I am very pleased to know you," Angie said, extending her hand. Sol pulled back, cautious of making any physical contact. Angie quickly withdrew her hand and moved to sit down at a safe, non-threatening distance. "I would like to encourage you to eat a bit more if you can. You seemed to enjoy that strawberry milk last night. Would you like some more?"

Sol remembered the taste of the milkshake. He remembered, too, the merry-go-round and the smell of popcorn. "Yes," he replied, "I would. And did I smell popcorn?"

"There *was* popcorn on the unit last night!" Angie said with congratulations in her tone. She was so glad Sol was recovering. "There is no popcorn now, because it's morning, but I could bring you some toast. Maybe some orange juice?"

"Thank you," he replied. As Angie left to get his breakfast, the thought of having breakfast seemed to calm Sol inside. Something normal. *Something...* He suddenly realized he was thinking, but not *thinksaying*. He was just thinking. Thinking about eating breakfast. For some reason he began to cry. He cried softly at first, and then a flood of tears came, wetting the front of his drooping pajama top. It was a cleansing cry, and it felt good, although he was relieved to have regained control of himself just in time for Angie to arrive with his breakfast tray. He was, after all, a Severson man.

Angie noticed Sol had been crying, but she wisely refrained from commenting. She sat the tray down on a bedtable in front of him, and as she uncovered the toast, she put Sol in charge of every aspect. Butter? Grape or strawberry jam? She brought an extra coffee so she could sit *with* him and so that he could have breakfast *with* another person. Sol was grateful for her company, and he was going to need a lot more of this sort of compassion in the times ahead. Soon, Sol would once again be bombarded with his various realities. Soon – all too soon – he would be forced to come to terms with his life.

# CHAPTER SIXTEEN

The ensuing two weeks of Sol's existence were spent on the E-Ward at St. Joseph's Medical Center, gradually reengaging with the world he shared with other human beings. There were many visits with helpful nurses and aides, continuing and gradually titrated pharmacological treatments, and helpful time spent in group therapy with other inpatients. There was good nutritional care and there were visits with Dr. Singh and with the unit psychotherapist. But looking back on it later, Sol would say that what gave him the most hope was his developing relationship with two people: Angie Corrales and Emma Prentiss.

Angie's kindness and gentle reassurance helped him to trust again. But one encounter really opened the door for Sol to move forward. Angie and Sol were sitting and talking over coffee, and the subject of Jan came up. Angie approached it cautiously, but Sol was ready to talk about it.

"We were so... normal!" he said. "Both working at our jobs, both involved with our daughter, Amy's, life. It's hard to imagine – even now – that it could ever have happened the way it did."

As she listened, Angie decided to tell Sol of her own connection to Jan. "You know, I knew Jan. She mentored me in my orthopedic rotation during nursing school. We really hit it off, too. If it hadn't been awkward with work schedules and such, I think we would have been really good friends. When I heard what happened..." A tear emerged from Angie's left eye, and when Sol saw it, he was completely bowled over. He reached across the table and took Angie's hand as his own tears began. They sat quietly, holding hands and sharing a moment of grieving together. And from that moment forward, Sol really began to come alive again. It wasn't only *him* who missed Jan. It wasn't only *his* sadness anymore. He had been connected with another person, someone else who really understood, someone else who knew Jan, who liked her and cared about her. It was an awful way to be connected to someone, but this tether of mutual grief became a lifeline, and it gave Sol the very traction he needed to begin pulling himself up out of the downward-spiraling vortex into which he had fallen. It would take time, but there had been a beginning with Angie.

As for Emma, that relationship was a little more complicated. Emma was Sol's secretary, and for him, it had initially been very difficult to see her outside of that role. About a week after he was admitted, Sol learned that Emma had tried to see him, but had been turned away. His first inclination was not to allow her to visit. Keep the boundaries clear, so to speak. But when he learned it had been Emma who had called to check on him, and that he probably owed her his life, Sol felt he would be remiss if he did not at least thank her. So, despite his reluctance, he signed the permission slip and the unit secretary phoned Emma to let her know it was okay for her to visit, which she did that very evening.

---

When Emma first approached Sol, it was in a large room, designated as a visiting area on the unit. The room had tables with straight-back chairs, suitable for card playing or sharing a coffee. There were also a couple of comfortable sitting areas with sofas and vinyl-covered chairs with ottomans. Sol was seated at one of the tables, hands folded, looking out the window at the bright, snowy day. As she moved closer to Sol, Emma almost didn't recognize him. *He's so thin!* she said to herself. She had the sudden urge to take him home and cook him a big dinner. But the thought of it almost made her blush. Emma had never thought of Mr. Severson in any romantic way. While she had always thought him an attractive man, he was her boss and that was the long and short of it. Still, seeing him this way, sitting there in casual clothes, wearing slippers, and so thin and sad and alone... it was as if she were seeing him for the first time. "Mr. Severson?" Emma said, quietly.

Sol looked up, and as he saw her cautious concern, he said, "They tell me I owe you my life. I hear in some cultures that means you are responsible for me now. Congratulations."

At first, she didn't know how to take that. Was he irritated with her? But when she saw Sol's face soften into a little smile, she breathed a sigh of relief. "I am so glad to see you, Mr. Severson." And she sat down in the chair on his right.

"I think once you are responsible for someone's life, you had better call him by his first name, don't you think?"

"Whatever you say, Mr. Se– I mean, Sol." Emma smiled a smile of nervous relief. It felt strange to call him Sol. "I tried to visit you a while ago, and their silly rules wouldn't allow it. But you have been on my mind and in my prayers every day. I didn't say anything at work. I thought you might not...well, I guess those privacy rules do have a purpose. But I am awfully glad you let me see you. You look good! But so thin! We need to fatten you up." The initial nervousness was wearing off, and the bubbly Emma was coming through as usual. Something about that vibrant, optimistic mien of hers suddenly seemed a little charming to Sol. Maybe he needed a little "bubbly" right about now.

They talked about work and who was doing what to whom at the office, and all the usual banalities. Emma did most of the talking. Sol, for his part, while glad to have some company, was ready for Emma to leave about fifteen minutes into their forty-five-minute visit. He just didn't have that much to say, and he never did have patience for the complexities of others' personal lives. When Emma finally made noises about leaving, Sol managed to thank her for coming, and for her discretion at work, and of course for her calls to check on him and to the sheriff's department. She really had saved his life, and he knew it. He just wasn't sure at this point whether that was a good or a bad thing.

After Emma left, Sol experienced a sudden surge of anxiety which he could not explain. He had not particularly looked forward to her visit, for a variety of reasons. But when she showed up, he found himself initially glad, buoyed up by her eagerness to see him. Then, as their visit proceeded, he couldn't wait for her to leave. Now that she had gone, one would think he would be relieved, but instead he felt this terrible anxiety, deep in the pit of his stomach. And that empty loneliness – that dark, deep pit of despair. He wasn't in it anymore, but it was looming all around and over him like a tornadic wind, whirling with the debris of his life and threatening to batter him to death with it. *How can you hate being alone and hate being with people, all at the same time?* he wondered. It was a conundrum, a puzzling maze, and it was going to take time to figure it out.

# CHAPTER SEVENTEEN

It was on a bright, cold January 14th – a Tuesday – that Sol was dismissed from St. Joe's. He made sure to find Angie before he left, and in an uncharacteristic show of emotion, he found himself embracing her with a thankful hug, his eyes welling up with grateful tears. He hadn't cried very easily his whole life; Severson men just didn't do that. Even at Jan's and Amy's funeral he managed to restrain all but a few tears, counting that as some sort of stoic success. But for some reason, as he faced this separation, his eyes refused to belie his emotions. The tears felt right and good, and Sol was not ashamed at all.

Angie wished him well as she handed him his discharge plan. Plans for follow-up care included a referral to the therapist Jan saw all those years ago, and a scheduled appointment with Dr. Singh, as well as an ongoing prescription for his antidepressant medicine. So, with a small satchel of his belongings in hand, Sol took a $40 cab ride back to Oakton Lakes. Back to reality.

As he made the trip home, it occurred to him he hadn't been outside for the last three weeks. It felt surprisingly good to breathe in the freezing cold air and to see his own exhalations clouding forth. It even felt good to be in the traffic again. Something about the noise of it seemed adverbial to his act of homecoming.

But while he was glad to be out of the hospital, the thought of going home to that empty house lurked in the back of his mind, irking him. It wasn't so much the fact of being alone there which was disturbing, it was facing all the work he knew it would take to make the house habitable again. And then there was his job. There were about six weeks left of his six-month leave of absence, and some decisions had to be made. Sol was deeply appreciative of the company's generosity in granting him so long an absence, and he felt he owed them a large debt. The only way he knew to repay that debt would be to return to them a fully functioning, productive employee. But right now, the thought of trying to face the work demands seemed simply overwhelming. He was still fragile; both the doctor and Angie told him not to go back to work for a while. And he refused to go back before he was ready, because he would absolutely *not* do mediocre work. He owed Argenta much more than that. If he couldn't perform at a high level, he wouldn't go back at all. There was plenty of money; both he and Jan had opted for $1-million-dollar life insurance policies, and with the double indemnity clause, that amount doubled. In addition, they had another million-plus dollars in investments (Sol was good at what he did). So, staying or going: it was another conundrum, and one he knew he couldn't avoid for long.

As the cab pulled into the driveway of Sol's home, he was surprised and pleased to find the driveway and walkways had been cleared of snow. He paid the cabbie and pushed the security code into the box beside the garage door. As the door opened, he saw his Honda, but it was bright and shiny clean, not at all the way he left it. Beside it was a Volvo with an Ohio license plate. *Maura?* he said, quizzically and nearly aloud. He hadn't seen or spoken with her since she returned home after the funeral. He moved quickly to the door which led into the kitchen hallway, but it opened before him as he got to it. And there, standing two steps up with that toothy grin, all grown up and with her arms opened wide, was Maura Severson Matz.

"Welcome home, big brother!" she said, and she jumped down the two steps into the garage, nearly knocking Sol over with a big bear hug. It made him think about his encounter with little Maura on the merry-go-round, and of the time he found her when she got lost. He hugged her deep and long, and the tears that he cried for Angie earlier that morning found another *raison d'être*.

"How..."

Maura interrupted him, "How did I know you were in the hospital? Well, a little bird told me. Your secretary, Emma, is quite a wonderful person. She found my number in your contacts list and called me. She told me everything that happened, and that she imagined you might need some help. So, I took some time off and came to your rescue. I must say, Sol, you really did need some help. This place!" Sol remembered the awful shape the house was in, but sensing his embarrassment, Maura said, "Well, I've never met a man who could survive without a woman to take care of him, so don't feel all alone. Anyway, it's been way too long. We need some bro and sis time."

Sol could not have agreed more.

As they went into the house, the first thing Sol noticed was the kitchen. It was spotless! It looked just the way it did when Jan was still there. It had never been Jan's "job" to keep the house in order. They shared the duties. But after her death, Sol just lost the ability to care about it. It sure was wonderful to see it back like it should be. As they walked into the family room, Sol was relieved to see the clock was in its usual place on the wall. And all the mess that had piled up on Jan's desk was gone. There was a pile of papers with a little sticky note on top which read "To Do." There was a smaller pile of papers alongside the first, labeled, "Sol needs to sort." Everything – the whole house – felt welcoming and new. And Sol could not have been more appreciative. He turned around and hugged Maura again, picking her right up off the ground with the strength of gratitude.

"Put me down!" she said, "You're going to break my neck. Or your own!"

In fact, the sudden pain in his lower back made Sol think she was right. Maura was a little meatier than she used to be, and he had lost a lot of strength, too, especially in the past couple of months. He let her down, and looking right into her eyes he said simply, "Thank you."

"You are very welcome. Now why don't you go get freshened up, and I'll pour us a couple of drinks, and we can talk. Is it still scotch?"

A scotch sounded great, but he thought better of it. "Maybe just iced tea for now."

"Coming right up," she said, and she turned to head into the kitchen.

Sol found his bedroom as immaculately clean and orderly as the rest of the house. He laid his little bag on the bed and felt the need for the bathroom. *I guess I have to actually go in there now,* he said to himself, a little amused. After relieving himself, Sol stood before the vanity and caught a glimpse of himself in the mirror. His appearance was a bit unnerving to him. His hair, while clean, looked unkempt. The skin on his neck appeared fleshy, not taut like usual. Even his ears seemed to hang lower. His shirt fairly hung on him as though draped on a hanger in the closet; nothing to fill it out. And his face looked unshaven, even though he had used the plastic razors they gave him at the hospital. *Never could get a decent shave out of one of those*. He rubbed his face with his hand, stretching the loosened flesh all around, and he decided to break out his good Dovo straight razor.

He soaped up his face and let the water run hot, till the steam billowed up from the sink. He pulled a washcloth from the cabinet (which he noted was filled with clean linens – thank you Maura), wetted it and applied the hot cloth to his face, luxuriating in the warmth of it. Then he worked up a good lather with his horsehair brush and worked it into his skin, being sure to cover every inch. The razor pulled evenly over his scruffy stubble, its carbon-steel blade effortlessly cutting through the rough facial hair. After the shave, Sol again soaked his washcloth in hot water and held it against his face, feeling just a bit more alive in the process.

Another look in the mirror: *not too bad*. He pulled a comb through his hair, patted both cheeks a few times with enough energy to make a slapping sound, and headed back out to sit down with Maura.

The iced tea was sitting on the coffee table beside Sol's brown leather chair near the fireplace. Maura was sitting on the sofa adjacent to Sol with her feet tucked in under her. Sol walked in and sat down, taking a big gulp of the tea. "Feel better?" Maura said. "You look better, even if you are skinny as a bean pole," she laughed.

Then she looked right at him. "Sol, why on earth didn't you call me?"

Sol didn't know what to say. What finally came out was, "I don't know, but probably the same reason you never called me after Jan and Amy died. Sometimes you just don't know what to say."

The brutal abruptness of that response hurt a bit, but

Maura realized it was nonetheless true. She and Sol had been raised by the same people in the same environment, and in their family there never had been much in the way of intimate conversation. Feelings were considered annoying intrusions on the real business of life, which was hard work and the pursuit of something called the American Dream. All those old adages about "making sure our kids have it better than we had it" were never more faithfully applied than in the Severson family. And when things got rough, like when their mom's appendix burst and she nearly died, or when the economy fell apart back in 1981 and Sol's dad nearly lost the house, never a word was spoken about feeling down or defeated or worried. The response of his parents to any negative emotion was always the same: get busy. Find something to do. Don't waste time feeling sorry for yourself; there's always someone worse off than you are.

The result of all this was the raising of two highly productive adults, each with a solid work ethic and a good record of achievements, but who had not the slightest clue how to be compassionate toward others; even when so inclined, they simply lacked the language for it.

"But you're here now, and that means more than any phone call could ever have meant," Sol said, regretting the way his answer probably sounded to her.

"So... how are you? What happened? I mean, if you want to talk about it..." Maura said, cautiously.

"Yeah, I don't mind talking about it. I guess it's pretty hard to explain, though." How could he possibly explain what happened, what was real and what was fantasy, what it all meant, when he wasn't totally sure himself? "I kind of went into a deep, dark place, I guess. I really don't know any other way to describe it. I wasn't able to distinguish what was real anymore. While I was...," how should he put it, "out of it, I did see you as a little girl on a sort of merry-go-round. You told me..."

Wide-eyed, Maura put her hand over her mouth like she'd seen a ghost as she interrupted him. "I told you I'd always looked up to you, and we talked about the time I got lost and you found me on your bike."

Sol's mouth hung open like a broken gate, and for a moment his breath was whisked away. "How in the world could you know that?"

"I had a dream," Maura said. "I was wearing my favorite little white and blue dress, and we were at the carnival in Tomah. But this time you were the one who was lost, and I told you I would tell you stories. Is that what you remember?"

"Yes!" Sol said, flabbergasted. "I was out of my head, psychotic, dreaming or whatever it was, but that is almost exactly what happened. How in God's name..." The invocation of God's name somehow changed the tenor of the whole conversation, but he continued. "How could this possibly be true?"

"I don't know!" she replied. "Too weird!"

"When did you have this dream?" Sol asked, intensely.

"The night after your secretary Emma called me. That very night I had this crazy dream. I interpreted it as something to do with worrying about you, I guess. I told Max about it, and he said the same thing: probably just an expression of my being concerned about you." Max was Maura's husband, who worked as a sales manager for Goodyear in Akron, which, no doubt, gave him an inside line on the interpretation of dreams, Sol thought to himself.

Sol never did like Max very much. What was interesting to Sol was how many times and in how many ways Emma's name continued to pop up in this unfurling mystery that was his psyche. He made a mental note to think more about this fact later.

"So... what do you think this means? What happens now?" Sol was becoming more and more intrigued.

"Well," Maura began, "I dunno, Sol, but maybe somehow we got..." she paused, trying to find the right word, "...well, connected some kinda way. I can't explain it any more than you, but maybe we should just follow the dream. Maybe I should tell you stories, things I remember about you and our family."

And with that simple suggestion, it was as though a light had begun to shine. Maura had arrived four days prior to Sol's discharge, so she had to return to her work at Sterling Jewelers back in Akron by the end of that week. But in those three days, an entire history began to unravel, both for Sol and for Maura. They talked more than they had in their entire lives up to that point. They shared all kinds of stories and remembrances, things from their childhood and the years leading up to college. They talked about their aunt and uncle, about their dad's parents, and about the mysteries surrounding their mother's family in Minnesota, who they both could remember visiting only once. There were things that Maura knew that Sol either didn't know or didn't remember, and the same was true for some of Sol's recollections. Each story shared was like opening a present they were not expecting to receive. Between them, they pieced together over those several days a sort of patchwork family quilt with a bunch of material missing, and it made them want to fill in the blanks.

GATHERED

That Friday, as Maura packed up to leave, Sol felt an unusual longing for her to stay. He had been too long estranged from Maura, and this time they had spent together made that abundantly clear. As he loaded her things into the back of her Volvo, Sol put his hands on Maura's shoulders and looked her squarely in the eye, "We need to keep this going."

She agreed, and she threw her arms around his neck and hugged him hard. "I will. I promise," she whispered in his ear. Sol said he would, too, and he truly meant it. As Maura backed out of the garage to the turnaround, she waved one more good-bye to her brother and drove out of Oakton Lakes to find the tollway back to Ohio.

# CHAPTER EIGHTEEN

When the phone rang at Emma Prentiss' apartment, she heard Sol's voice on the other end before she even picked up the receiver, and when it really was Sol, her startled reaction spilled over like new wine. "Mr. Sever– I mean, Sol! Hi! How are you doing? I'm surprised to hear... I mean, it's good to hear from you!" She felt the blood rushing to her cheeks as she heard herself gushing with school-girlish babble.

"I wanted to thank you – again – for being so kind and taking such good care of me," Sol said. "Calling my sister was the best thing you could have done for me – for us both, actually. Thank you."

"I'm glad it helped. I felt a little funny, looking through your desk and everything, but I just wanted to make sure somebody in your family knew what was going on, and the only person I ever heard you mention was your sister, Maura. You never did talk that much about personal stuff, your family, you know... So, Maura called you?"

"Actually, she came all the way out here from Ohio and helped me get the house back in order, and we spent a lot of time talking. We hadn't done that in many... well, never. It was good to catch up."

"I'm really glad, Sol. That's so important. Like I always say, my family is my life. So, how are things going now? How are you feeling?"

The question set him back on his heels a bit. *How am I feeling?* He was not used to assessing his emotional state. "Well, I guess I'm feeling hopeful," he replied, "at least a little bit. And I'd like to take you to dinner. You pick the time and place."

This time it was Emma who was taken aback. Sol had always been so formal and detached at work, it was astonishing to find him so personable and inviting. "I'd love to!" she said. "How about your favorite place, Sevilla? Maybe next Friday?"

*Sevilla... the last time I was there I was with Jan,* Sol thought, sadly. *But I told her to pick the place...* So, he replied, "Sevilla will be great. You're right, it is my favorite place. I'll pick you up at home about 7:00 p.m., okay?"

Emma replied, "Seven o'clock will be great. I'm at 4932 Regent St., Apartment 7A in Mundelein. See you then!"

As he hung up the phone, Sol felt a sudden twinge of regret. *Do I really want to go on a date with my secretary?* He hadn't really thought of it as a "date," although it could easily be construed as such. But any reluctance he felt was quickly pushed aside by his overpowering gratitude for all Emma had done. She showed a level of concern and caring for him that Sol could never have expected, and which he sorely needed. Dinner was the least he could do for her.

———————

On Wednesday that week, Sol had his first appointment with Dr. Sally O'Keefe, the therapist Jan and he had seen all those years ago when she was struggling with depression. As he drove to the office building in Naperville, Sol was swallowed up by a flood of memories, painful, anxiety-provoking memories, memories which contained all the sadness and the anomic, eddying chaos that constituted those troubled times with Jan. He had to steel himself for the prospect of opening that office door again; he recalled feeling such relief when he walked through it for the last time in the other direction. But accompanying the horrid, dark memories was the memory of relief and healing Jan had found in Dr. O'Keefe's presence, and it was that memory that steadied Sol's hand as he reached for the door handle.

The office was just as Sol remembered: a private practice with Dr. O'Keefe the only occupant. There was not even a secretary, only a small seating area. On the beige wall was a doorbell next to the inner office door. A sign above the doorbell had a large, black arrow pointing downward: Please press the button only once on arrival. Dr. O'Keefe will be with you shortly.

As Sol pressed the button, he noticed that the place looked exactly the same. The same location, the same neutral colors, the same chairs. Something about that consistency calmed him inside. Everything in his life had certainly changed; even the world itself had undergone a few metamorphoses in the last ten years, it seemed. But this was a place of some stability.

He had only waited a few minutes when he heard the door handle click, and Dr. O'Keefe emerged. "Sol? Please come through." She motioned for Sol to sit in the chair where Jan used to sit. "It's been near ten years, i'nit?" Her Irish background showed itself in her euphemistic language and in her greying red hair.

"Yes, almost," he replied. "You look nearly the same as I remember you."

"Well, I could show you all the wrinklies, but there's no need of that," she said with a smile. "I reviewed the file they sent from St. Joseph's, so I have a good, thorough understanding of your recent illness and history. You've really been through it, han't ya? I'm so very sorry about Jan and Amy."

*Jan and Amy.* Just hearing their names these days always seemed like a life sentence. "Thank you. I guess it took more out of me than I thought. I got kind of lost for a while. And after I got better enough, I suggested your name for the follow-up plans. So here I am."

And so, their healing journey began. Dr. O'Keefe listened as Sol recounted his experiences in the past year at home, at work, and during the time of his leave of absence. He told her what he could recall of the dreamy, detached state he was in at home, and of the wind tunnel place and the time on the merry-go-round, and of his "conversations" there with Maura and with Uncle George. He told her of Angela Corrales and how she became his link back to reality, and of his gratitude to his secretary, Emma, for going out of her way to take care of him, and of the recent reunion he had had with Maura, stopping short of recounting their "connection." He was concerned that little detail might seem a little too crazy. Dr. O'Keefe wrote it all down, just as Sol related it.

As the hour was coming to a close, the doctor sat quietly for a moment, pondering all the information he had given her. Finally, she said, "We have some work to do, you and me. I think you should come weekly for a while. Does this time and day of the week suit you?" Sol said that it did. "Then I'll see you next week, same time." And with that, Sol headed for the door. As he got to it, he turned and said, "Well, Doc, can you make any sense of my crazy mind?" He said it glibly, but inside he really wanted to know.

She looked up over the top of her reading glasses, and a playful smile showed some of those "wrinklies" as she replied, in full Irish brogue, "Well, as we say in Ireland, you may have been a half-bubble off true, but you're a far cry from full loopers. We'll figure it out, you and me. See you next week."

And as Sol left the building for the parking lot, he felt some relief that she said he was not "full loopers," whatever that was. And he was already looking forward to next Wednesday.

# CHAPTER NINETEEN

As Friday arrived, Sol and Emma were having similar feelings of trepidation about their dinner date, but for quite different reasons. For Sol, beyond his usual introversion and dislike of small talk, the prospect of spending time with his secretary placed him squarely before the conundrum of his potential return to Argenta, a topic on which he remained undecided. He could handle hearing about what was happening with the company, with Henry Mellison, with the other account reps, and so forth; but Sol worried about what he would say if she posed the ultimate question: When are you coming back?

Emma, on the other hand, was excited to be spending time with Sol away from work. She always relished time with people, and this situation was no different. But *her* nervousness was about how to be in this new relationship with her boss. She had initially wanted only to help him, and her phone calls when he was in crisis were simply an extension of her work role. She had never considered any further relationship with him, he, being a happily married man, and she, his subordinate. The idea of friendship never occurred to her, let alone anything beyond friendship.

Yet Emma could not deny a certain attraction she felt on their last encounter. She tried to ignore it, to dismiss it as merely compassion and caring for someone who was hurting. After all, that had always been her nature. Even when growing up in her hometown of Rockford, Emma was always drawn to those who were left out or hurting in some way. One time in the third grade, a new little girl named Susie Flynn was being picked on in the school cafeteria because of her bright red hair. Emma saw the mean treatment, and she went right to her. She said, loudly so the others could hear, "I think your hair is pretty." Then she linked arms with Susie, and they walked over to a different table and ate their lunch together. They became fast friends and stayed that way for years.

Yet, when that phone call came and Emma heard Sol's voice, it was no sense of rescuing she felt. What she felt was a spark in a place deep inside her. It was a place that had only been moved that way one other time, and that was when she met her former fiancée, Mike Althus. She was in her mid-twenties at the time; having just finished business school, she was still living in Rockford. She had certainly had other relationships and flirtations, but nothing came of those. When she met Mike at a singles dinner party, he lit that spark.

Mike was strong and handsome and very solicitous. He told her he was a combat veteran, that he had served two deployments in Iraq, and that he was recently discharged from the Marines. The fact he had served his country impressed Emma, and they occupied one another's attention the rest of that evening, and quite often for the next several weeks. They fell in love quickly, and just over six months later they were engaged, with the wedding date set for the following summer. But then things changed.

Mike had told her the truth about his time serving in the Marines, but not all of it. The full story was that while he was in Iraq, he got into an altercation with a superior officer that landed him in jail. He beat the guy so badly that he required hospitalization. There was a court martial, and while Mike was able to negotiate a general discharge, he was required to serve the remainder of a one-year term in Federal prison before regaining his freedom. He had only been released from prison less than a month before Emma met him.

He had been so courteous and kind through all the time of their courting. Emma saw little or no indication of the fiery anger seething just underneath the surface, nor did she see evidence of his hair-trigger temper; somehow, he was able to keep it all contained. But it seemed as soon as that ring was on her finger, Mike became more and more possessive, as well as more and more controlling. He was quick to become jealous, a tendency which Emma tried to see as his way of protecting her, but soon enough it became clear that Mike's jealousy was all about him.

They were at a high school reunion party together one Saturday evening, and one of Emma's friends from high school was there. His name was Evan Daniels, and he and Emma used to regularly hang out together back in the day with a group of others who were into art and English and history. That evening Emma and Evan and several others were talking and laughing, and when Mike saw them from across the room, he came over quickly, grabbed Emma roughly by her wrist, and said, "Come on, we're going."

Emma pulled back, saying, "What do you mean? We just got here! What's the matter?"

Mike wrenched her arm, pulling her behind him, and she cried out in pain, "Mike, you're hurting me!"

At this point Evan intervened, a fight ensued, and Mike knocked Evan unconscious. From that point on, Emma knew this was a dangerous situation. She gave Mike back the engagement ring and called off the wedding. He was remorseful, then angry, and he finally became so aggressively persistent with her that a restraining order became necessary.

Mike eventually moved out of state, but it took a couple of years before Emma was able to quit worrying about his return. Even now the occasional twinge of fear could still peek out from its closet in her mind and raise up phantoms of foreboding.

After her experience with Mike, Emma never again felt any sort of romantic urgings toward anyone. Until now. Until Mr. Severson suggested she call him Sol. Until he invited her to dinner. She told herself not to make too much of it; after all, he was probably just feeling a debt of gratitude for her calling to check on him. But that spark was there, and there was no denying it. And so, therefore, was the nervousness.

The appointed hour arrived and so did Sol, right on time, carrying a purple flowering plant. "I brought this for you. I thought maybe it would brighten up your desk or something."

Emma took the plant admiringly, "Thank you so much! That wasn't necessary."

"Some things you do not because they're necessary, but because you just want to," Sol said, remaining in the hallway.

"Would you like to come in, maybe have a drink before we go?" Emma said.

"Thanks, but maybe we'd better have our drink at Sevilla. The traffic…"

"Yeah, the traffic. Never seems to die down, does it? Well, let me get my coat."

And with that, they made their way out to Sol's spiffy-looking Honda (thank you, Maura) and made the twenty-five-minute drive to Sevilla.

When they entered the restaurant, Lorenz seemed to

have been waiting for them. "Mr. Severson! How wonderful to see you here again! It's been too long! Too long!" And Lorenz grabbed Sol's right hand with both of his own, sliding his left hand up to grasp Sol's forearm. It was a very warm greeting, one which Sol hadn't anticipated, although he probably should have. His association with this restaurant – and thus with Lorenz – went back over ten years, and Lorenz highly valued his regular customers.

"It's good to see you again," Sol said, and he was surprised to find himself truly meaning it. "This is my secretary, Emma Prentiss."

"*Srta. Prentiss, bienvenidos*. Welcome to Sevilla!" He kissed her hand with the elegance of Don Juan.

Emma liked him immediately. "Thank you very much, *señor*," she said.

"We have a special table for you, Mr. Severson, to honor your return to Sevilla. And *con permiso*, I have prepared a special family recipe for you tonight, a *paella* from Valencia that my grandmother's grandmother made. I also chose a wine specially to accompany this recipe."

"It sounds wonderful, Lorenz. I know it will be wonderful. Thank you very much," Sol said, a bit embarrassed by all this fanfare.

Lorenz motioned to a young woman. "Manuela will show you to your table, and I will see to the preparation of your meal. *Bueno provecho!*" And with that, Manuela (who was Lorenz's daughter-in-law, and who had a lovely, soft smile) led Sol and Emma to their table in the corner, by the window looking out over the currently snow-covered *terraza al fresco*.

They ordered before-dinner drinks, a single malt for Sol and white wine for Emma, and as they awaited their drinks, Emma (not surprisingly) spoke first. "I must say, I am very impressed by how well they seem to know you here. It seemed like the owner was actually camped out waiting for you to arrive."

"Yeah, it's a little overwhelming, but Jan and I…"

His voice trailed off, just for a second, as her name floated in the air between them. "Well, we used to come here pretty often. Lorenz is a truly wonderful chef. And the wine list here is quite amazing."

"Well, here we are!" Emma's usual effervescence came shining through. "You look great. Starting to put a little weight back on, aren't you?"

"Yeah, ten or eleven pounds, I guess. I feel stronger. I can't imagine what it must have been like to see me at the hospital," he said, hoping to keep the conversation away from Argenta.

"You were definitely thin," Emma replied, "but you still looked like you. I was just so glad to see you, I didn't care what you looked like," she said, recalling how she actually felt at the time. "But that was then, and this is now." She raised her glass in a toast, "Here's to now." They clinked glasses and Sol took a pull from his scotch. *Now…* he thought to himself. *What now?*

The evening progressed, with the meal proving to be just as amazing as Lorenz promised. The *paella* was perfect, with moist chunks of whitefish, scallops, calamari, mussels, and andouille sausage all seasoned with saffron and Spanish paprika in a risotto that absorbed and celebrated every flavor. And the whole dish was topped with two huge prawns, perfectly braised in shrimp stock. The wine was a lemony Spanish *blanco* – just a hint of sweetness in it – to balance the spice in the *paella*. Dessert was mandatory at Sevilla, and nearly always consisted of a melt-in-your-mouth *flan*, caramelized perfectly just before serving, and accompanied by an aperitif of hearty ruby *porto*. It was a truly wonderful meal, with enough left over for two large portions to take home.

Afterward, the bill folder was brought to the table and all it contained was a note which read:

> It was my pleasure to welcome you back to Sevilla.
> Please come back soon. Your friend,
> Lorenz Serrano Cortez, Propietario.

Sol was overawed, but he knew protesting would be useless, and maybe even offensive. So, he thanked Lorenz profusely, leaving a $50 tip for the waiter before they left.

On the way back to Mundelein, Sol suddenly noticed he was feeling very relaxed, with no hints of his earlier anxiety. And he realized why: all during dinner, not one word was spoken about Argenta or when he might be returning. Somehow, Emma just knew not to bring it up, which he found tremendously helpful. Sol hadn't felt this relaxed around anybody in a very long time, and he was grateful to Emma. *Again,* he was grateful.

They arrived back at Emma's apartment, and Sol walked her up to the door. Emma thanked him for such a great meal and told him she had a wonderful time. Then she invited him in for a nightcap. All the attendant associations which accompany such an invitation hung in the air like deep breathing in the freezing cold. An uncomfortable few seconds passed before Sol declined, claiming tiredness and a concern for how much alcohol he'd already consumed (which was all mostly true). Sol reached out his hand as he said, "Again, I hope you know how much your thoughtfulness has meant to me. I had a great time tonight, too. I haven't felt this relaxed in quite a while."

Emma took Sol's hand. With her other hand she pulled him down to kiss him on the cheek. "Maybe we should do this again sometime," she said, with a genuine smile.

"Maybe we should," he replied. She entered the security code and opened the door. Looking back with one more smile, she said, "Good night, Sol," and the door closed.

All the way back to Oakton Lakes, Sol was thinking about newness. *Here's to now*, he thought, nearly saying it out loud, recalling Emma's toast. Then he did say it, with a sense of hope and purpose, "Yeah, dammit! Here's to now!"

Sol slept better that night than he could remember having slept in a very long time.

# CHAPTER TWENTY

Sol's weekly appointments with Dr. O'Keefe proceeded as planned, with the expected ups and downs in both process and progress. Along the way, he finally resolved the second of his conundrums when he informed Henry Melisson that he would not be returning to Argenta. Sol offered to repay Argenta for the four months' salary, and he truly wanted to do so. After Melisson declined the offer and wished him well, Sol made a $50,000 contribution to Argenta's Community Foundation, a non-profit charity dedicated to improving the lives of people living in lower income neighborhoods.

Dr. O'Keefe began to focus more and more intently on the topic of Sol's main conundrum: his apparently simultaneous desire and disdain for being with people. The emotional process eventually centered on Sol's relationship with his father, which came as no surprise to him. Throughout his life, Sol had been confronted with sad or difficult memories of his dad, and he had evolved a sort of automatic response, tending to push away those memories by focusing instead on some current issue that needed his attention. Dr. O'Keefe shut off those avenues of escape. She pushed Sol directly into these memories and the feelings associated with them. The result was some very difficult and painful sessions which at times became nearly as terrifying for Sol as the dark cloud that had enveloped him prior to his hospitalization. Two such sessions were especially important.

The first had to do with the summer before his senior year of high school when Sol worked as a summer help stockman for the company where his dad worked. Sol told the story to Dr. O'Keefe.

"I learned to operate a forklift, which I used to fetch pallet loads of machine parts from the rows of four-level storage frames in the warehouse.

"One day one of the older workers tried to take down a pallet from the highest level, and he misplaced the forks, unsettling the load and nearly bringing down the entire row of shelves and several hundred tons of parts. It would have been a terrible loss, both in terms of inventory and structural costs, not to mention the possibility of someone getting killed in the process."

"What happened?" Dr. O'Keefe asked, intrigued.

"Well, when I saw what happened, I quickly got another forklift and maneuvered it to the other side of the shelving unit. I raised the fork carriage until it made contact with the uppermost beam, and then I very slowly moved the machine forward, lifting the carriage just enough to provide support and push the load back toward its correct position. The other worker was then able to grab the load, lift it, and safely lower it to the shop floor."

"Wow!" Dr. O'Keefe retorted. "That was pretty quick thinkin', wa'nt it?"

Sol looked down at the floor. He said, "Yeah, the warehouse manager, Frank Prine, heard what happened and praised me up and down for what I did. He said my actions averted what could have been a disastrous situation."

"And you just a young buck, too!" the doctor said. "I bet your dad was proud, eh?"

Sol looked at the floor again. "Yeah, well..." His gaze moved to the office window, to some place far away. "My dad was, of course, on the road again, but when he returned from his sales trip, I knew he heard about it at the office. I kind of hoped he would bring it up at the supper table, but he didn't mention it at all. So, I asked him, 'Dad, did you hear what happened this week at the warehouse?' He never looked up from his plate."

"What did he say?" Dr. O'Keefe queried.

Sol's face steeled against the memory. Dr. O'Keefe gently patted his hand as she said, "It's okay. Tell me the rest of it."

"Well, what he said was that he heard I was out there playing hero, and that Frank Prine said, 'Your kid is gonna outshine his old man.'

"Then he looked right at me and said, 'Why couldn't you just be grateful for the job and do what you're told? Why'd you have to show me up?'

"I didn't know what to say. I guess I just sat there dumbfounded."

"Is that all?" Dr. O'Keefe dug deeper.

Sol's cheeks began to swell red with the memory, and tears filled his eyes as Dr. O'Keefe said, simply, "Go on."

"I never meant to show anybody up. I just reacted to what happened at the time. But he said he had told Frank Prine I was needed at home the rest of the summer and that I couldn't go back to work there anymore."

"What did you do then, Sol? And how did you feel inside?" Dr. O'Keefe pushed him.

At that moment, Sol had felt like bashing his father's head in. He even remembered looking around the room for something he could use to do so. The memory came spewing out in words, "I wanted to kill him!"

"But you didn't kill him."

"No. I said, I'm sorry, Dad. I meant no disrespect."

Sol still recalled the sight of his father, cutting through his meatloaf, his eyes still buried in his gravy, and his father's facile reply, "That's all right boy. You didn't know. Go on up to your room, now."

"I kept waiting for my mother to say something, but she just sat there looking sad. I remember I went upstairs and cried like a baby."

Dr. O'Keefe said, softly, "Like you're doin' now, eh? It still hurts, duhn't it?" Sol just fixed his gaze on the floor.

The doctor wrote a few notes to herself, and then she said, "You know, Sol, you didn't owe your father that apology. That's a hard thing to do, to apologize to a man just to keep from killing 'im. It's quite a sacrifice, in fact. Maybe even heroic."

Just then the timer clicked its notice of the hour's end, and Dr. O'Keefe said, "We are gettin' into it now, son. Don't let's wait for next week. You come back and see me again tomorrow. Let's keep at it. Same time work for ya?"

Sol agreed and left without another word. But as he left the building, he felt like a new light had been lit. It was a faint light, but it was there. Much like when he and Maura had begun talking. Something new was happening. He dried his eyes and went home.

––––––––––––

The next day brought the second and most painful session. It dealt with the time of Sol's father's death, and it began with Dr. O'Keefe's simple question, "So what is your most crystal-clear memory of your father?" Sol responded immediately, "The day he died." Dr. O'Keefe said, "Tell me about that day."

"Me and Jan had been married about two years and had

just moved to the Chicago area. Mom called and said that my father had suffered a stroke and he was 'not good,' which was the local vernacular for dying. We hurried back to Tomah to be with Mom and to say good-bye to my dad. Maura wasn't married yet and she had just finished college, so she was still living at home. We all arrived at the hospital just as the doctor was emerging from the hospital room. He said Dad was comfortable, but he was in and out of consciousness, so if we wanted to talk to him, we should do so sooner rather than later. A nurse came out and said, 'Mrs. Severson, he's asking for you.'"

"Mom went in and Maura and I sat in the visitors' lounge, waiting our turn to see him. Jan sat by herself in a corner chair, leafing through some magazines; she said she didn't want to intrude. After about ten minutes, my mom came in and said, 'Maura, he's asking for you.' Maura got up right away.

"I asked my mom if Dad knew that Jan and I were there. She said she told him. She said he was just used to Maura being around, so he asked for her first. 'He'll ask for you next,' she said.

"About ten minutes passed before Maura returned. She was teary eyed, and she hung onto my shoulder and said, 'Mom, he wants you to come back.' My mother left immediately, and I held my sister as she cried.

"Finally, after another few minutes, my mother came back and said, 'He's gone.' She and Maura both fell into my arms, crying. I just stood there staring out the window into the parking lot. I remember thinking, *Here I am holding the two people my father wanted to see, with my wife watching from a distance, and I feel absolutely nothing at all.*"

Dr. O'Keefe sat quietly, reflecting on all Sol had told her.

Finally, she said, "Sol, your father didn't deserve to see you, but he needed to, and he needed to a long time before that day in the hospital. It's time you stopped paying his debts."

———————

It took several months of work, but with Dr. O'Keefe's help and the continued support of the antidepressant medication, Sol began to come to terms with the fact that his father had never given any indication he was proud of his son, or that he was pleased with him, or even that he loved him. What had eventuated for Sol was a lifelong search for approval and appreciation, one which resulted in a pattern of high achievements in school and at work; none of which ever satisfied him at all.

The surprising outcome of all this therapeutic work was a realization that Sol really never knew his father. Since he didn't know who his father was, he didn't have enough information to know what his father might have been thinking and why. So, to address this problem, Dr. O'Keefe wrote a sort of behavioral prescription: "Go find out. Do some in-depth family-history research. Try to learn from others what sort of man your father was, not only during your years with him, but before those years. What sort of boyhood did he have? What was the nature of his relationship with his parents and teachers? What were his hopes and passions and fears? Who was he, deep inside, and how did that affect the man he became as your father?"

The therapy sessions were suspended for two to three months, during which time Sol was to do his research. He was free to call Dr. O'Keefe with any questions or concerns, or just for support, but their next face-to-face appointment would await the completion of his research.

Sol continued nurturing the relationship he had begun with his sister Maura. They exchanged phone calls on a weekly basis, as well as texts and emails of any memories or ideas either of them had about their family. Emma Prentiss also became as much a part of Sol's family explorations as Maura, though in a different way. Sol and Emma began to see each other more regularly, for dinner or movies or coffee. Sol became more and more relaxed with Emma, and she noticed it and told him that she liked him that way. While they were not physically intimate, Sol truly appreciated the affection Emma showed toward him, and he started to show the same to her. Little gestures – a touch on the arm, a notecard of friendship for no special reason, even the simple action of asking her about how she was feeling or about her family – all these things were never part of Sol's interpersonal repertoire before, not even in his relationship with Jan. But it seemed life was evolving, and so was Sol.

There was one moment of serious difficulty. That moment occurred when Emma's old fiancé, Mike Althus, showed up unexpectedly at her door while she and Sol were having dinner together. The knock on the door seemed to startle Emma, who was not expecting anyone. "I'll get it," Sol said, hoping to dispel whatever was bothering her. He opened the door. "Yes? May I help you?"

The man at the door was stocky and very well built, wearing an olive T-shirt and a brown aviator jacket. "I'm here to see Emma."

"And you are..."

"Mike. Mike Althus."

On hearing his voice, Emma's gut seized up. It was him.

He'd come back. She feared she might be sick to her stomach. *How did he get in? What was he doing here?*

Some time ago Emma had told Sol about her history with Mike, and that she still worried sometimes what he might do if he returned. Sol stood squarely in the doorway, keeping the door open only enough for conversation, and he told him in no uncertain terms that he was not welcome on Emma's property. Mike was not immediately willing to accept this fact, saying he wanted to hear it from Emma's own mouth. So, while never breaking eye contact with Mike, Sol called out, "Emma, do you want this guy on the premises?"

Emma said, loudly enough for Mike to hear, "No, I don't want him here, and if he won't leave, I'm calling the police."

Sol said, "See? She doesn't want you here. Now I suggest you leave before she calls the cops."

Mike's eyes were smoldering. He took a half step closer to Sol in the doorway as he said, "Okay, I'm leaving. Maybe I'll see you again sometime." It was a menacing retort, one which Sol hoped was bluster, but which he sensed might not be. *Well, it's been a lot of years since my last fight; maybe I'm overdue*, he thought to himself, and he made a mental note to be a little more intense with his workouts, maybe add in a little kickboxing.

After Althus left, Sol found Emma was just shaking. Sol put his hand on her shoulder, and she grabbed him and began to sob. Sol held onto her, surprised that he felt so protective of her. He couldn't help thinking back to that awful night in the LHS gym and how his words of reassurance to Jan and Amy were lost in a hailstorm of bullets and blood. Whatever else happened, he would never let that happen again. "It's going to be all right," he said, holding Emma's head against his chest. "We're going to call the police and let them know this guy is back in town. He probably won't stay around long."

They did phone the police, and Emma was able to speak with a Sgt. Baker, who remembered her earlier problems with Althus. Sgt. Baker assured her he would try to locate him and warn him off. He also asked her to make sure she was extra careful for a while when leaving home or work. He suggested she buy a can of mace or pepper spray and keep it in her hand until she got safely into her car or into the building. Emma thanked the officer and promised to do as he suggested. After a week went by with no further incidents, Emma began to relax a bit and so did Sol. But she kept that pepper spray close at hand everywhere she went.

———————

With his nascent hopefulness, Sol was beginning to feel a sense of urgency to begin his family research work. It seemed to him that the continuing of his newfound openness and hope was somehow tied to getting the answers he needed about his father. So, he decided he should go back to Tomah. He thought a good place to start might be with his Aunt Christine. She knew Sol's father well. Maybe Sol could stay with her on the farm for a while. He could help out if there were chores to be done.

As he considered calling her, Sol worried about two things. First, he worried about leaving Emma alone after the incident with Althus. When he spoke with Emma about it, though, she was all for him going. "You need to do this," she said, and she assured him she felt good support from the local police.

Secondly, Sol worried that Aunt Christine might see his "self-invitation" as an imposition, especially since he had shunned nearly every family contact for all these years. But when Sol phoned and proposed the visit, Aunt Christine was thrilled! She told Sol he was welcome to stay as long as he liked, and that she looked forward to seeing him.

The next day Sol arranged for the care of his house for the next several weeks. He didn't know how long this might take, but he was determined to pursue his father's ghost as long as necessary. That's how he began to refer to this quest on which he was embarking: chasing his father's ghost. Although, he already had the ghost. What he was looking for was flesh to put on the bones. After packing about a week's worth of clothing, Sol backed the Honda out of the garage and drove off to find his father.

# PART THREE: SPRING

It's spring fever. That is what the name of it is.
And when you've got it, you want – oh, you don't quite know
what it is you do want, but it just fairly makes your heart ache,
you want it so!

Mark Twain, *Tom Sawyer, Detective (1896)*

_____

Spring is when you shake the curtains, and pound on the rugs,
and take off your long underwear, and wash in all the corners.

Virginia Cary Hudson, "Spring," *O Ye Jigs & Juleps! (1962)*

# CHAPTER TWENTY-ONE

Christine Severson loved her life in the country. She had always felt safe there, so much so that she never locked the doors to her house until her neighbors insisted she do so after George died. So insulated was Christine's life, that she was truly amazed when she learned how very few people live out their adult years in or near the place of their birth; she simply assumed everyone did. She herself had never ventured farther than a few hundred miles from the farm on which she was born, a now derelict place set into the hills in Norwalk Township, about 20 or so miles from the Severson homestead.

The farm Christine now owned belonged originally to George's grandfather, Eiver Severson, who, along with his wife, Cornelia, established a homestead in the late 1800s of about 80 acres of farmland and another 80 acres of woodland. The original log house served as the Severson home for the first forty years or so until it was replaced by a frame home made of sawn lumber and beautiful glass windows. The new house was purchased from a Sears catalog for $1800, and was shipped by flat car to Sparta, whence it was trucked to its current site for assembly. A huge old manor of a home, it had four bedrooms but only one bathroom (a second bathroom was finally added years later, long after the original owners had died).

Eiver and Cornelia had two sons, Delbert and Christian, and a daughter, Maybelle. Maybelle was sickly and never made it past her third winter. Christian was kicked by a horse when he tried to hitch up a plow rig, and although he didn't die right away, his resulting fits of violence and seizures became impossible to control, and he lived out his years in a sanatorium until he died at age forty-one.

Delbert grew into adulthood on the farm on which Christine now lived. He learned from his father how to work the land, and together they built a very profitable and handsome farmstead. New buildings were added over the years, a chicken-coop first, followed by a farrowing house for the sows. Corn cribs and silos were built, and as the farm slowly modernized, the production and prosperity grew steadily.

Along the way, Delbert met Helen Olsson at a church social, and they courted for a little over a year before they were married in the local Norwegian Lutheran church. In short order, their union produced three sons, one of whom, named George, was to become Christine's husband.

When George and Christine got married, George's father helped them buy a double-wide mobile home, which was situated about 150 feet away from the home place. By the time Delbert Sr. died, George and Christine had the twin boys to raise, so Helen suggested she trade living spaces with the growing family. She moved into the smaller home where she remained until she had to move to the nursing home in town. George and Christine visited her often and brought her out for Sunday dinner most weeks until a stroke took her at the age of ninety.

The farmstead really was a beautiful, serene place. The wooded areas surrounding the farm were comprised of a mixture of hardwoods including maple, ash, and several varieties of oak, a lot of alder, poplar, and locust trees, the ubiquitous white birch, and a number of pine species (mostly jack pine and blue spruce). It was a paradise for bird watchers and wildlife lovers, as well as for aspiring hunters of deer and turkey. And while the former bustle of the farm's more active years was past and gone, the land still produced lavishly for those who rented the acreage. "The land," she remembered George's father Delbert quoting his own father, "the land will always take care of whoever works for it."

Christine had rented out the double-wide a few times over the years, usually to a young couple just starting out. But the last renters moved out about a year ago, so Christine decided to let Sol stay there during his visit. She thought this would afford him some privacy, and they could get together during the days and evenings up at the home place for coffee and meals and visiting. She got the little home all gussied up, putting clean sheets on the queen bed and fresh linens in the bath and kitchen. She ran the furnace fan and opened the windows to bring in some fresh air, and by the time Sol came rolling up the end drive, the house was about as welcoming as anyone could want.

As Sol stood up, stretching from the long drive, he saw Aunt Christine rising from her wooden glider chair on the front porch. "Sol!" she said, with a wave and a welcoming smile. Her face was wrinkled, but they were wrinkles of love and happiness. Her hair was nearly all white, with only a hint of the former Norwegian blonde remaining. Sol knew she was in her late eighties, but she seemed amazingly spry and fit. Still, he strode quickly up the front porch stairs so she wouldn't have to negotiate them, and when she wrapped her arms around him in a warm embrace, Sol felt an intensely genuine welcome in her arms. He felt at home.

Christine offered him some fresh lemonade, which he quickly accepted. As she disappeared into the house to fetch the drinks, Sol sat on the bench beside the glider and looked the place over. His view from the porch was spacious, both in actual and temporal visage. He could see the rows of growing soybean bushes in the field on the other side of the end drive, and the wooded hills beyond. He could see the huge oak tree in the front yard, flanked by two smaller, but still enormous, maple trees on either side. He could see the large black crow above the field, and he could hear its complaining as it lumbered away from the attacks of several barn swallows, defending their territory. The smell of fresh haylage was in the air, as was the faint remnant of recently sprayed fertilizer.

Just by itself, in the present moment, it was a nearly perfect scene of calm for Sol. But along with the senses of the moment came the attendant memories of this place. He could see where the big tractor-size inner tube once hung from the branch of that oak tree, and he could hear the shrieking laughter of the children – himself included – as they clamored on that makeshift swing. He could feel the splash of water balloons as he and his cousins battled for bragging rights. He could see the flat place in the yard where the picnic table once sat, extended by the addition of a couple of folding card tables and covered with a couple of variously patterned tablecloths. He could see the table loaded up with plates of burgers, bratwurst, hot dogs and buns, accompanied by huge bowls of potato salad and beans and coleslaw, and all the extended family seated around it. He could see the homemade ice cream bucket, and he could feel his muscles aching from the challenge of continually turning the crank on that freezing can to set the cream. It was all there – right there in front of him.

Christine brought out a tray with a large glass pitcher filled with lemonade and two glasses filled with ice. She made the lemonade from real lemons and sugar, even including some lemon slices in the serving pitcher. She poured each of them a glass, and when Sol took his first sip, the taste perfectly reified the reverie he had been experiencing there on the old porch. He tipped the glass back and drained it hungrily. And he wanted more.

"I'm so glad you asked to come and see me," Christine said. "But I have to admit I was awfully surprised to get your call."

Sol looked out at the yard, thoughtfully, and he replied, "I've been ill." And he then began to tell his aunt about all that had happened after Jan and Amy were killed. He told her everything, omitting no details.

"So," he concluded, "here I am, looking for information about my father. And I couldn't think of a better place to begin than with you."

Christine sat quietly for a moment, pondering all she had heard. "Well," she said, "I guess it should come as no surprise to me. I used to see the way your dad treated you sometimes. He was never abusive – at least I never saw him being abusive..." Her recollection was halted by a sudden awareness that, unbeknownst to her, Sol's dad might actually have *been* physically abusive, and her quizzical tone invited a response.

"No," Sol responded, "my dad never hit me."

The relief on Christine's face endeared her to Sol even more as she continued. "It seemed like more a kind of competitiveness. Whether it was wiffle ball or badminton or horseshoes, or even just roughhousing in the yard like dads and kids do, he seemed to always make sure he came out on top. I remember seeing you cry sometimes at having been defeated so badly."

"Yeah, and then he would try to smooth it over by saying stuff like, 'no hard feelings, it was just a game' or something like that. I even remember him scolding me for crying, like he was embarrassed I was being such a baby."

"Yes," Christine said with a sigh, "I remember that, too."

"I hadn't thought about that in many years," Sol said meditatively. "And I guess that's why I'm here. Like Maura told me in the dream, I need to hear stories to remind me of who I am."

"Well, I'm glad you are here," Christine replied. "I really am."

"Me, too, Aunt Christine," Sol said, placing his hand on hers and patting it gently. "Me, too."

# CHAPTER TWENTY-TWO

When Sol awakened the following morning, he was in the midst of a vivid recurrence of his dream about the boat and his father and his boyhood friend, Tim. His father had that same sullen look on his face as Sol remembered from the earlier dream. But this time it was Sol and Tim who were in the boat; his father was on the shoreline, dolefully watching. Sol again hooked a fish, and it was a big one. As he fought with great difficulty to haul it in, Tim couldn't get his line out of the way. The result was a tangled mess, with Tim's rod eventually snapping in two and Sol's fish escaping. Sol looked over to the shore to see his father, laughing. It was a mean, derisive laugh, and Sol was furious. He started to make his way to shore and to his father with the intent of letting him have it, but the shoreline kept getting farther away, and his father's laughter got even more intense. By the time Sol woke up, he was feeling so enraged that he was afraid of what might have happened had he ever gotten that boat to the shore.

Sol arose and washed the sleep out of his eyes, trying also to wash the angry dream from his mind. He made himself presentable and set out to find Aunt Christine. As he approached the house, he could smell the wonderful aroma of bacon frying and fresh baked bread. By the time he hit the back porch he was salivating like Pavlov's dog. "Sure smells great in here!" he said as he opened the door and entered the homey, huge kitchen.

"How do you like your eggs?" came the response.

"Over medium is fine," he said.

"Over medium it is. There's fresh biscuits keeping warm in the oven, and hot coffee on the stove. Help yourself."

"You didn't need to go to all this trouble," Sol said, suddenly aware of the effort it must have taken to prepare such a repast, especially by someone in her mid-80s.

"Oh, nonsense! It feels good to have somebody to cook for again. Sit down and make yourself at home."

Sol grabbed the oven mitt he saw on the counter and took the bowl of baking powder biscuits from the oven, placing it on the trivet he found on the table. He poured himself a cup of coffee and sat at the place Christine had already set for him. He broke open one of the biscuits and buttered it. Real butter. He couldn't remember the last time he tasted anything so good. "Oh my god is that good!" he mumbled, his mouth still full of the salty bread. He noticed a jar of homemade strawberry jam and added a generous spoonful to the other half of his biscuit. It was absolute heaven.

Christine stepped over with a plate of bacon and eggs for Sol and one for herself. As she sat down, Sol was eagerly picking up his silverware. He was stopped short by his Aunt Christine's soft voice: "Be present at our table Lord. Be here and everywhere adored. These mercies bless and grant that we, may feast in paradise with Thee. Amen." Sol didn't remember it till that moment, but that was the table prayer they used to say before every meal when he was a kid. He hadn't heard it in years, but for some reason it sounded wonderful. Something about the sound of his Aunt Christine saying that prayer comforted him in a way he could not have anticipated, and which he didn't even try to understand. What he realized was that he felt immensely grateful to her for saying it.

"Thank you," Sol said, and he meant it sincerely.

"It's no good to forget our manners," Christine said. "We get all this wonderful bounty every day; the least we can do is say thank you." Sol pondered her words. He had not experienced much in the way of gratitude for quite a while. "Well, dig in!" Christine said. And he did.

It was a wonderful breakfast, and Sol insisted on helping clean up the dishes afterward. When all was put back in order, they both sat down again at the table with cups of coffee. Christine seemed eager to get on with addressing Sol's questions. "So, what can I tell you?" she said.

"Just anything you remember about my dad, I guess. You first met him when he was still a boy living at home, right?"

"Yes, that's right. He was George's younger brother. His older brother, Arne, had already gone off to the war when George and I started going out together. Arne was eighteen, George was sixteen, and your dad was thirteen. Arne got killed in the battle of Midway, exactly one year after I met George. And one year after that, George enlisted, too. Just like Arne, George left to fight when he was eighteen years old. I worried I would never see him again. But four years later, he came back to me. Three months after he came home, we were married.

"Your dad was expected to help his father on the farm, but his heart was never in it. My George loved farming; he was born to be a farmer. But not your dad; he dreamed of one day owning a business in town. I don't think it's too strong to say your dad really hated farming. He even tried to enlist in the Army when he was seventeen. He said he wanted to follow his brothers, but I think he mostly wanted to get away from the farm. After your grandfather wouldn't let him go, there was a lot of bitterness between them. And then when your dad just up and left, well..." Christine's voice trailed off as her eyes searched the rolling hills for the right words, "... I guess they never got together much after that."

Sol had been stirring his coffee mechanically, listening to his aunt's recollections. He was surprised to learn that his dad had such difficulties with his own father. It made him sad. "Dad never told me all that," Sol said.

"After he left, your father never really came back to the farm at all until after your grandfather died. George and I had been living here and working with your grandpa on the farm, and as his dad got older, George was taking over more of the work. He wanted your dad to come and help. He needed his help, too, but it was more than that. George used to talk about how much he hoped he could find a way to bring your dad and their father back together, and that maybe if he could convince your dad to come and help him with the farm, it might be a way to begin healing that relationship. But your dad never would come."

"He didn't go to school right away, did he?"

"No. He spent a couple of wayward years as a longshoreman out on the river. It was dangerous work, tending to those heavy barges of coal and salt and grain; your grandmother worried about him constantly. But I guess he needed some distance from the farm and from his father, and the river was the way he got it."

Sol had seen a couple of pictures of his dad working on a barge, but all his dad ever said about it was that he worked on the river after high school before going off to business college. Sol never knew the reasons behind it all. He had no clue of his father's deep anger. And as the realization of it set in, Sol almost began to feel sorry for his father, which, for Sol, was a very uncharacteristic feeling. A very uncharacteristic feeling, indeed.

As Christine continued to introduce Sol to his father, one thing began to be clear to him: Deserved or undeserved, bearing the disapproval of one's father was a Severson family tradition.

# CHAPTER TWENTY-THREE

Sol and his aunt carried on their conversation all the rest of that day, punctuated by breaks for iced tea and ginger cookies, lunch, and an afternoon nap for both of them, her in her bed and Sol in a big hammock strung between two posts in the shaded front yard.

Supper consisted of grilled steak from a locally butchered beef, grilled sweet corn, and an apple/peach pie with ice cream for dessert. *One thing's for sure*, Sol thought to himself, *if I hang around here very long, I'm sure going to put some weight back on!*

The next day Sol decided to drive in to Tomah. It had been many years since he spent any real time in the town of his boyhood years, so about mid-morning he headed out. He parked his car and got out directly across from the local bank, which was much the same as he remembered. With its concrete fascia and columned supports, it still looked like the architectural equivalent of some sort of armed guard. The old Rialto movie theatre was gone; folks now went to see movies at the AMC 8 out on the north side, built there amidst the newer construction and its fast-food and strip-mall sycophants. Sol used to love going to see movies at the Rialto. There was even an old pipe organ there, which had been retired from use many years before, but whose continued presence still whispered of times when moving picture shows required some sort of manual sound accompaniment.

The old drug store on the corner was also gone, replaced by chain stores and a Wal-Mart. Sol remembered ordering chocolate sundaes and sweet cherry limeades at the soda counter in that old drug store, just down the street from where the theatre used to be. Mr. Wilson was the pharmacist, and his daughter, Marj, used to work up front, along with a string of high school kids over the years. The space was being used now for a consignment and resale store.

Up the street a few blocks was the old watering hole called "The Other Place," where Sol drank his first legal beer. It's also where he played pool and darts and got on bowling and softball teams. Had college not lured him away, Sol might easily have become one of the "usuals" at The Other Place. The name derived from an acrimonious history in Tomah.

Many years earlier, there had been only one bar in the downtown area: Paul's Place. Paul Johnson was the owner, and he lived above the bar in a spacious three-bedroom apartment with his wife and two children. After Paul had been accused of inappropriate behavior with a local high school girl, people began to shun his business, even driving to other towns to enjoy their beer and pretzels.

As it turned out, Paul was acquitted of the charges against him, but the local scuttlebutt was that he had simply gotten away with it, that he beat the rap on some technicality with the help of a smartass lawyer. Soon, good old American enterprise took over and a guy named Nick Drumm opened up a different bar, located about eight blocks away from Paul's Place, and he called it "The Other Place." Of course, his business was an instant success. Less than two years later, Nick had to expand due to all the customers he was serving. Paul's Place hung in there for a few more years, chiefly patronized by an aging, mostly alcoholic group. When Paul died, so did Paul's Place.

It was close enough to lunchtime that Sol decided to

visit his old hangout and have a sandwich and a beer. He opened the front door and was amazed at what he saw: the place had not changed a bit! Same dark wood bar, same brass foot rail, even the barstools looked like those he remembered, with tubular steel frames with a dark-red vinyl covering on the seats and the seatbacks.

As Sol looked up, he could see there were a lot more trophies than he remembered. There were rows of them, displayed on the wall above and behind the bar, the collected spoils of many years, won by the efforts of well-lubricated patrons representing "their bar" in the social milieu of the Monroe County area. Bowling trophies, softball trophies, pool league trophies; there must have been about seventy-five of them decorating the walls, proclaiming their feigned, shiny, small-town glory.

Sol sat at the bar at the place he used to sit, close to the pool tables in the back. There were a few others at the bar, nursing their draft beers, some with a shot glass alongside, some eating their lunch. Sol hadn't really noticed the person sitting two seats down from him, but when he glanced around the bar, he noticed the guy looking at him. He was wearing a jean jacket and a badly stained T-shirt, and his hair looked tousled and not particularly clean, though not as dirty as his hands. Sol looked up to see the bartender, who said, "What can I get you?"

Sol settled on a draft Old Style beer and a patty melt with deep-fried cheese curds. As he glanced around again, Sol saw that the guy had moved over closer to him. "How're you doin'?" Sol asked, trying to be friendly.

"It IS you!" the voice next to him almost shouted out. "Sol Severson! Don't you recognize me? It's Tim!"

Sol looked closely at the disheveled man alongside him,

and suddenly it was plain as day: there right next to him was his boyhood friend, Tim. After all these years, here, standing right beside him at The Other Place in Tomah, Wisconsin, was Tim Massey. Amazing. They both stood up grinning and shook hands. There was the inclination to embrace, but Tim stopped it by saying, "I'm pretty groaty from work. Don't want to get your fancy clothes all greasy." So, the two of them sat back down and tried to figure out what to say to one another.

As the childhood friends reminisced, updating one another on a lifetime of divergent experiences, Sol tried to be engaging. But there were few points of mutual experience. Tim had been married twice and divorced twice. He had three children, now in the custody of their respective mothers, and most of his income was devoted to child support. He had never left Tomah, never pursued an education, and had little interest in what might be happening in the larger world. It was becoming painfully obvious that they did not have enough to talk about. Anything Sol thought of to say about his own life risked the appearance of bragging, despite his intent. Tim knew about Jan and Amy's deaths, but all he could say now was how sorry he was, and he meant to send a card but never got around to it.

Thankfully, Tim had to return to work – something about polishing the heads on a 396 Chevy big block or something. They exchanged contact info and agreed they should try to get together again before Sol went back home. But as he left the bar, Sol was hoping his reunion with Tim was done.

Sol noticed he was starting to feel a little overwhelmed on the way back to his car. Walking along the sidewalks of downtown Tomah, the place felt alien to him. There were still people on the sidewalks, still moms holding their little ones' hands; people still *lived* here. But Sol's memories just didn't jibe with the way the place looked and felt. Added to this strangeness was the recently acquired information about his father's history, and now this unlikely reunion with Tim (Sol couldn't help but recall the disturbing dreams involving them both). With everything swirling around in his head, he might as well have been in an episode of *The Twilight Zone*.

Returning to his car, Sol began to feel the anxiety of this place. This place of his father, and of Sol never feeling good enough. This place from which he and Jan had escaped over twenty years ago to build a successful career and a home of their own in Oakton Lakes. He was trying to process it all, but the whole experience was too much. He was almost beginning to long for his safe wind-tunnel place, and the realization terrified him.

But as Sol drove out of town and headed back to the farm, he began to relax. It seemed the closer he got to the farm, the more sense he was able to make of everything. And just as he was about to turn down the road leading to the Severson farmstead, he realized it: visiting his boyhood and its attendant relationships was just that – a visit. He could come and go from that place and those times. And another thing: the difficulties of those years were and are part of a whole life – his life – and they were accompanied by a great many good memories and good people. *It isn't either or. It's both and.*

As he turned onto the graveled end drive leading to the house, Sol resolved to make a call back home that evening. He needed a reality check. He thought about calling Dr.

O'Keefe, but he wanted to make sure Althus wasn't causing any trouble for Emma. Also, he really needed to hear Emma's voice. And as he came to *that* realization, a smile relieved his face. *Here's to now...*

# CHAPTER TWENTY-FOUR

Mike Althus sat at a computer desk in a library in Elgin. The incident at Emma's apartment had prompted a visit from the local sheriff's department, a humiliation which was deepened by an escort out of town and a warning not to return. He was more than a little irritated at having to kowtow to some local Barney Fife whose ass he could most certainly kick, but he swallowed back his anger and capitulated to the deputy's order. One thought sustained him on his demeaning drive out of Mundelein: this would certainly not be the end. Emma was *his*, and nobody was ever going to take from Mike Althus what was his. So now he was doing some detective work.

After he paid the user fee on one of the internet background search sites, Althus learned Sol's name through a vehicle license plate check, which then enabled him to find a plethora of information on Emma's new friend, Delbert S. Severson, III. He learned about Sol's employment at Argenta. *So that's it. She met him at work.* The report listed Sol's education at UW-La Crosse, that he was a CPA, and that his birthplace was Tomah, WI. He found Sol's address in Oakton Lakes and the number of years he had lived there. He learned that Sol had a wife named Jan and a daughter named Amy, and that there was no record of arrests or lawsuits. *Figures,* he thought to himself, *Mister Clean. Except he's a married man, screwing my woman.* The anger rose up his neck, burning his ears.

After the background check, Althus did a name search in the local newspapers, and he read all about the tragedy at Lancashire High School and how Jan and Amy had been killed. *Okay, not married. Tough break, but that doesn't mean this pussy accountant gets to move in on my girl*, he thought.

As he left the library with his newfound knowledge, Althus went back to his car to find somewhere safe to park and sleep for the night. After buying a six-pack of beer and a hot dog at a convenience store, he found a spot in a wooded area behind a grocery store in Elgin and pulled up beside a stack of pallets. He wolfed down the hot dog and opened one of the beers, nearly draining it. His head was filled with Emma Prentiss, and the thought of her with this Delbert guy infuriated him more and more. He quickly finished the first beer and opened another. And as he tipped back the can, he began to imagine what he might do to Emma's boyfriend.

———————

After another wonderful supper with Aunt Christine, Sol had a headache, so he excused himself and went back to the mobile home for the evening. As soon as he got settled, he got out his cell and phoned Emma, who answered almost immediately. "Emma?"

"Hi!" she said, her usual cheerfulness lifting Sol's spirits right away. "I was hoping you might call. How goes the searching?"

"It's been quite a couple of days. Too much to say over the phone, but I just wanted to make sure you were okay. Any more trouble?"

"Nope. Not a peep. I've been keeping aware like they told me, but I haven't seen any sign of Mike. Don't worry, I'm fine."

"I'm glad to hear it. And I want you to know..." (he debated saying it, but it came out anyway) "...I was very much looking forward to hearing your voice."

Emma stifled a shriek of glee as she shoved her fist in her mouth and turned the phone away from her. "You were?" she managed to sound calmly surprised. It was all she could do to hold back her joy in hearing Sol talk to her this way. She was starting to fall in love with him, but she didn't want to seem too eager and risk pushing him away. Besides, she had just received a very sobering reminder of what happened the last time she got attached too quickly. She was determined that would never happen again.

"Yes, I was," he replied. "I just wanted you to know that."

"I'm glad, Sol. Like I said, I was really hoping you'd call. When do you think you'll be coming back home?"

"I'm not sure. I think I'm going to hang around a little longer. It's been awfully good being with my aunt. I forgot how nice a person she was, and I'm learning things I never knew about my dad. I'll let you know as soon as I can."

"I'd appreciate that. I'm kinda getting used to having you around." As soon as she said it, she worried it was too much.

But Sol responded, "I know, me, too. Stay safe. Good night, Emma."

She hung up the phone and let out a squeal as she flung herself down on the deep, cushy couch in her living room. She pulled a throw pillow over and hugged it across her torso, thinking what it might be like if Sol loved her. It was a comfortable feeling, and one which stayed with her throughout that evening until it carried her off to sleep.

---

When Sol opened his eyes in the morning, his headache

was gone, and he felt at peace. He slept with the window open beside the bed, and now the sound of birds singing and the earthy smells of the fields invited him into awareness like a soft caress. He lay there a few minutes, remembering his conversation last night with Emma and enjoying the calm.

After a shower and a shave, Sol headed up to the house to find a note left for him on the kitchen table. Christine had her weekly Wednesday morning meeting at church, so Sol was to help himself to breakfast. After some toast and coffee, he sat down at the computer desk built into the wall adjacent to the kitchen. He called up a map of Wisconsin and zoomed in on the western side of the state. There was his college town, La Crosse, maybe an hour away. It was where he and Jan met and fell in love. He clicked on it and was rewarded with a slew of marketing pop-ups, one of which advertised houseboats for rent. He thought about his dad having traveled the river, and the idea intrigued him enough that he clicked on the link. The pictures showed quite a variety of different-size boats, all with onboard facilities and air conditioning. They weren't cheap; Sol learned that renting a houseboat for most of a week would cost around $2,000, and even more for a larger craft. But it had been many years since Sol had even been on a boat, and the thought of piloting a boat down the Mississippi River alone was not appealing. He quickly dismissed the idea and returned to the map, zooming in on the river.

"Man, I forgot how massive this thing is!" he said out loud. He traced the Mississippi up to what is commonly accepted as its source, a lake in northern Minnesota called Itasca. Sol remembered going there on the one visit they made to his mother's family when he was a youngster. His grandparents were there, but for some reason, Sol had no clear memories of them at all. He simply recalled they were there, but no interactions, no impressions – nothing registered in his mind about them. They all drove up in two cars from the Twin Cities to Bemidji, and then another half hour or so to the place where the Mississippi begins to drain from Lake Itasca. Sol recalled the place was so narrow and shallow that people were walking across it. His dad had a sprained knee, so he didn't want to cross over the creek, but Sol wanted to try. The challenge was to make it across in twelve steps, which Sol did not accomplish on the way over, but did on the way back. He looked to his dad for approval, but his dad just walked away. *I guess I won that one, eh, Dad?* Sol mused, sadly.

Sol hadn't thought at all about his mother or her family for a long time. Aside from his grandparents' names – Thomas and Sharon Bakken, and the fact that his mother was an only child, there was a cloud of mystery about them. Sol's mother had always shied away from discussing her family, and without knowing the details, Sol grew up somehow intuiting this was a painful subject for her. He learned to leave it be. He did, however, see evidence of the troubles in his mother's family on one occasion. It was when her mother died, and the family went up to Saint Louis Park for the funeral service. Sol was fourteen years old at the time.

At the visitation, Sol noticed his mother standing in the reception line as the mourners filed in. Her father stood closest to the casket, then Sol's mother, but with Sol's father beside and behind Sol's mom, and always between her and her father. As Sol watched from across the room, never once did his grandfather approach Sol's mother or console her. Not once. Sol also noticed that his mother never approached her father the whole evening. Only when they first arrived did she go anywhere near him, and again, it was with Sol's father beside her, almost like he was guarding her. Sol couldn't explain it, but he felt a sense of danger that seemed to intensify the closer Sol's mother was to her father.

Of course, it was never talked about. Seversons did not talk about such things, and Sol's mother had eagerly become a Severson in every sense of the term. Just like a Severson, she put all such emotional issues up on a shelf somewhere, boxed up and sealed with packing tape, and then got busy. Regardless of her painful past, Morgan Severson loved her children and was proud of them. Sol knew that, and so did Maura. And that was enough for them. No need to go searching through any closets.

Sol continued his impromptu reminiscence, studying the geography of his family's history in the upper Midwest until his cell phone thrust him back to the present. The caller ID said "Tim Massey." Sol wasn't sure he wanted to answer the call, but he couldn't find a good enough reason not to. "Tim! How's it going?"

"I'm good. Glad I caught you still here. It was great seeing you again the other day, but that lunch hour was too short. I was wondering if you maybe wanted to come over for dinner. I bought a couple of real nice steaks. It'd be good to do some more catching up."

Sol *really* wanted to decline, but after all, Tim had bought the steaks... "Sounds great," he said, not meaning it in the least. They got the particulars established and made a date for the following evening. As the call ended, the anxiety he felt on his visit to Tomah fluttered in his abdomen once more, but then he remembered his new mantra: *it's not either or; it's both and.*

# CHAPTER TWENTY-FIVE

Sol spent the rest of the day with his Aunt Christine. After she returned from her meeting at church, they had a quick lunch and then headed out to the garden. It was a huge plot, with several rows of potatoes, a square patch of sweet corn, ten bushy tomato plants, and a dozen long rows variously sporting green beans, sweet peas, beets, cucumbers, zucchini, onions, green and red peppers, and kohlrabi. Sol was surprised how good it felt to work up a sweat and dig in the dirt. They hoed and raked and pulled weeds (which took the entire afternoon), and as they moved up and down the rows of growing vegetables, Sol and Christine talked back and forth, not only about Sol's father but also about Christine's life in west central Wisconsin. For some reason, Sol was surprised to realize how much she loved living here; it simply hadn't occurred to him that folks could *love* living in this place which he had so eagerly disavowed.

The following morning Sol volunteered to mow the lawn, which was about ¾ of an acre, including a portion along the road which Christine always kept trimmed for tidiness' sake. Even using Christine's John Deere riding tractor, by the time he finished the mowing and trimming, it was nearly lunchtime. A quick shower was followed by a lunch of hot beef and gravy sandwiches, which Sol hungrily devoured.

After washing the lunch dishes, Sol and Christine sat down again with glasses of iced tea. "I can't tell you how grateful I am for you taking me in like you have," Sol said.

"It really has been a pleasure having you here," Christine said in reply. "With George gone, and of course the boys, too..." Her voice trailed away, and Sol could see her eyes moistening. "Well," she took a deep breath and managed an enthusiastic smile, "it's just really nice having someone here to be some company. And especially family. Especially you, Sol."

Christine stood up and moved close to Sol's chair, pulling his head softly into her abdomen and hugging him with a true, motherly love. It was plain to Sol that she was missing her sons terribly. He put his arms around her waist and returned the embrace as he said, "Thank you, Aunt Christine. Thank you."

Sol sensed his aunt could use some time alone, so he decided he would head back to the trailer and take a nap. He lay down, thinking of the past few days, of his conversations with his aunt, of his time in Tomah, and of his reunion with Tim. His mind drifted back to Emma and Mike Althus, and to what that situation might bring. As his eyelids began to close, he realized his time here with Aunt Christine was nearing an end.

---

When he arrived at Tim's house that evening, Sol was startled to see it was the same house where Tim was raised. Sol had written down the address when Tim phoned, but it just didn't register at the time. But as soon as he turned onto Maple Street, he recognized it. *Wow*, he thought, *who lives in the same house he grew up in?* The memories came flooding in – times spent riding bikes, comparing baseball cards, building forts in the apple orchard just a few blocks away, avoiding encounters with all the "cool kids."

Sol had stopped along the way to buy a nice bottle of red wine to have with the steaks, and as the front door opened, Tim grinned his greeting, "Wine, eh? No flowers? Come on in!"

Sol was amazed at how different Tim looked. His hair was combed neatly, and he was dressed in khakis and a white polo shirt with the green and gold "G" of the Packers football team affixed on the shirt pocket. His hands showed no signs of Tuesday's grease and grime. *He could be mistaken for a resident of Oakton Lakes*, Sol thought. "You clean up pretty good!"

"Yeah, I don't spend my whole life rolling in the grease," Tim said. "You want a beer?"

"Sure. You're still living in the same house after all these years? How did that happen?"

"I inherited it after Mom died. Andie didn't want it; she lives out in Massachusetts now, and she married a lawyer. They've got more money than God." Andie was Tim's little sister, Andrea Jean. "And with the child support and all, I really needed a house I could afford, so here I am. Weird, huh?"

"Yeah, life's a funny old dog, isn't it?" Sol looked around the place. There were several large fish mounted on the wall. "You apparently still like to fish."

"If I could live out on the water, I probably would do it. You know what they say, 'a bad day fishing is better than a good day working.' Here ya go." He handed Sol a bottle of Old Style. "No micro brews in this house. Just the old stand-by."

Sol took a big swig. "Tastes really good and cold." In truth, Sol wasn't much of a beer drinker, but there was something appropriate about drinking an Old Style beer in Tomah.

"Yeah, if it weren't for fishing and my karate, I don't

know what I'd do," Tim said, as he settled back into his big easy chair.

"Karate?" Sol sounded surprised. "You mean, chop chop, breaking boards and jumping up and kicking someone in the face, karate?"

Tim laughed. "Yeah, pretty much. I achieved seventh degree black belt last year, which is the highest in the dojo where I train. Keeps me focused and balanced."

"And in good shape, I imagine," Sol said. "I'm impressed. You never took much interest in sports when we were kids."

"Nope. It took a few years before I got lured into the karate world. But it's been very good for me. Still, if you ask me most days, I'd rather be fishing," Tim laughed and took another swig of his beer.

"I was looking at a map of western Wisconsin and the Mississippi the other day. I had forgotten how much water there is up here. And that river! It's huge!"

"Yeah, it is. Fun to go out and fish on, too. Lots of backwater areas you can get into with a johnboat. Catch crappie all day. Come on out on the patio and I'll throw the steaks on."

They had a good dinner. The steaks were excellent, and the wine didn't hurt a bit. The two men talked with a greater ease as the evening proceeded. Maybe it was being together in that house after all those years, or maybe Sol was just learning to relax, but he was really glad he came. Tim was not in the same social class Sol was used to, but surprisingly, that seemed to Sol a good thing. No pretense. No "neighborhood associations." No hierarchy of parking spaces. Just two childhood friends, all grown up and reminiscing over a steak and some wine.

"You know," Tim said, "I'm taking off next week to go fishing on the river. I get a week of vacation each year, plus a day for Thanksgiving and Easter, and usually some time off around Christmas, too."

Tim seemed to be trying to impress his obviously more successful friend with the lavishness of his earned leisure, and Sol picked up on it: "That's a lot of time off!"

"Too bad you can't come with me. It would be fun. But I'm sure you have to be leaving soon. Have to get back to all those numbers and spreadsheets, I suppose."

Like a bolt out of the blue, it hit Sol right in the head. "No, I don't. You really want company?"

Tim bolted right out of his chair, bent over and looked Sol in the eye, and got this big grin on his face. "You mean you'd come with me?" That same old boyhood expectation was evidently still there, the expectation of being rejected and left out, of being judged inadequate or goofy or not cool enough, it was all right there in that shocked, excited, amazed look on Tim's face.

"Yeah, I'd come with you!" Sol replied. And then he proceeded to tell Tim about his father's history of working on the river, and how he had clicked on a houseboat rental place, and how he dismissed the idea because of not being familiar with the river or with boating, and because he didn't want to do it alone. As Tim listened, he got more and more excited. But suddenly a cloud appeared in his otherwise chirpy demeanor. Sol saw it and asked him, "What's wrong?"

"Ohhh..." It was a groan of resignation. "I was just going to drive over and fish a few times. No way I could afford half of a houseboat rental."

"How about this," Sol said. "How about I rent the

houseboat, and I hire you as boat captain and river guide. I'll pay you with room and board and Old Style. You supply your own bait. Whaddya say?"

"You'd do that?" Tim asked, incredulously.

"Yup, I would. Is it a deal?"

Tim's big grin slowly crept back into place, and he stuck out his hand: "It's a deal!" And then they shook on it. An outside observer would have thought they looked like two little boys who had just planned some fanciful and daring exploit: grinning from ear to ear, they virtually jumped up and down shaking on it.

The rest of the evening was spent in a flurry of planning. Lists were made for everything: fishing tackle, food, beer (and other various libations), clothing, emergency supplies – nothing was left out. Sol would arrange for the houseboat rental, and they made a plan to leave early Saturday morning and return the following Thursday or Friday. When Sol finally left at about 10:30 p.m., he could not remember having ever felt so excited about anything in his whole life.

# CHAPTER TWENTY-SIX

The alarm on the nightstand by Sol's bed rang at 5:00 on Saturday morning, but he was already in the bathroom. He had packed the car the night before with everything for the trip, and rather than disturb Aunt Christine so early, they had said their farewells the night before. He promised her he would stop back to see her after his time on the river. He also phoned Emma to let her know what was going on, and even though he knew she was anxious for his return, the idea of his river trip seemed to excite her as much as it had him. *Gonna have to keep that girl around*, he said to himself after hanging up the phone.

After double-checking that he had everything, Sol headed out the door and into town to pick up Tim, who he found ready and waiting on his front porch. Since the houseboat was equipped with a fully functional kitchen, they decided to buy food at a local market after taking possession of the boat. This made packing pretty simple: clothing and fishing tackle, plus a few other necessities, all loaded up easily in about fifteen minutes. They were on the road by 6:00 a.m. and planned to arrive at the boat rental company by 7:00.

Tim brought a couple of travel mugs filled with coffee, and Aunt Christine sent along some sandwiches and fruit, all of which the two men pursued with vigor as soon as they were on the road. There was little conversation at first, the earliness of the hour not lending itself to small talk. But as the sun rose higher behind them, they began to wake up more, and Tim broke the silence. "So why were you so anxious to go with me out on the river? In fact, come to think of it, you never really told me why you came up here in the first place. Why did you?"

Sol took the question in, cautiously. "Well, what should I say..." How much of the true motivations for his visit should he share with this childhood friend, a man who, for all intents and purposes, he had only met a few days ago? Sol knew he had to respond, and after considering a variety of ways he might do that, he decided he might as well just tell Tim the truth. And so he did. All of it. For the next thirty minutes, Sol related his entire experience of the past year or so, beginning with the murders of his wife and daughter and including his descent into a psychotic depression. He told Tim about the weird dreams involving his dad and himself and Tim, and he told him about Emma Prentiss and his run-in with her former fiancé, Mike Althus. He told him about Dr. O'Keefe, and he even told him about the strange experience he had with Maura and how she knew the content of his dreamlike conversation with her before he told her about it.

Tim listened intently to the whole story as he ate the second half of a roast beef sandwich and sipped on his coffee. Finally, Sol finished up by telling Tim the reason for his trip: to mine the treasure trove of his Aunt Christine's memories of his father, in hopes of understanding him better and making sense out of this lifelong difficult and confusing relationship with him. "So.... whaddya think? Still want to go out on the river with me or did I scare you off?" He phrased the question much the same as when he had asked Dr. O'Keefe if she thought he was nuts.

"You're not gonna go all Norman Bates on me, right?" Tim said, feigning apprehension.

Seeing the teasing smile on Tim's face, Sol responded, "I don't know of any quicksand pits along the Mississippi, so I think you're safe."

"Seriously, though," Tim said, as he looked right at Sol, "who wouldn't have some trouble after what you went through? I can't imagine standing there right next to anyone getting killed, let alone my own wife and daughter. And as for your dad, I always thought he was kind of an asshole."

"You did?" Sol said with obvious surprise. "I don't recall you saying anything when we were kids."

"Well, I didn't know what to say. Of course, I didn't see you with him all that much, 'cause he was gone so much and all. But I remember thinking he used to like to put you down in front of me, sort of make you look silly or embarrass you or stuff like that. Never could understand that. And it made me uncomfortable, too, kind of like me being there made it worse or something. Come to think of it, I guess seeing the way your dad treated you made me appreciate my own dad more, 'cause all he did was tell everyone how proud he was of me. Even though I don't think I did all that much to make him proud; I never was that good in school or even in sports. But he still bragged about how proud he was of his kids, me and Andie both."

Somehow it helped Sol hearing Tim's recollections of Sol's father. It was validating to realize he wasn't just being a crybaby or overreacting. These things did happen, and they were noticed, and they weren't appropriate, and Sol's feelings were justified. As they continued westward on I-90, Sol was beginning to think this entire trip was unfolding like a road map to a place not yet known. The map was being gradually revealed as the journey progressed, and as he followed it, he was learning just how far this journey might take him. "Thanks, Tim. It's good to know you understand. It really helps, and I'm glad I'm here."

"No problem, buddy," came the response, along with a slap on Sol's knee. "Now let's get ready to do some fishing!"

"Almost there. Let's do it!" he replied.

Tim turned on the radio and tuned it to the local classic rock station just as they began to play the Eagles' "Already Gone." It was perfect. The two of them sang along at the top of their lungs, especially at the chorus: *And I'm a—ll-ready gone; And I'm fee—eee—eelin' strong. I will si—ing this vict'ry song. Woohoo hoo! Woohoo hoo!* And that song was followed by another and then another, and before they knew it, they were pulling into the driveway of Sid's Houseboat Rentals.

Sol eased the Honda up to the office. A scruffy, bearded man wearing a red-and-black plaid shirt-jacket and a tattered, floppy fishing hat emerged from the tiny, log-sided building. Sol and Tim got out of the car, and Sol said, "Can I assume you are Sid?"

"That would be me," the old man said as he shook first Sol's hand and then Tim's. "You got here right on time. Ready to get out on the river?"

"Pretty close," Sol said. "I assume there's some paperwork that needs signing, and then I hope you can direct us to the closest grocery store so we can buy some supplies."

"Yup. The IGA is just down the road a piece. Come on inside and we'll get you all legal." Sol signed all the appropriate documents and issued the check for $2,500, which included a $500 refundable deposit against any non-insured damages to the boat. Sid led them out along the wooden pier about 100 feet, passing several other boats until they got to where their particular houseboat was docked. It was a very nice craft. There were deck chairs up front and some built-in lounge sofas in the back, and a stainless-steel gas grill was mounted on the front side rail. As they stepped on board, Sid showed them all the safety equipment, life vests, boating regulations, and tie-downs. Then he opened the insulated sliding glass door to the living compartment, which included a seating area, a satellite dish-connected television, and a full galley with refrigerator, gas range, and microwave oven. He showed them the controls to the wall-mounted A/C unit before leading them down a narrow hallway to a full bath with shower and two bedrooms, each with a queen-size bed. "Very nice!" Sol said. "Very nice, indeed!"

As they returned to the front area, Sid showed them a small staircase that led to the pilot's station, and he oriented both men to the ship's radio and to the controls for the engine. He had both men read the procedures in case of emergency, and both signed an agreement that they understood them, after which he dropped two sets of keys in Sol's hand. "I hope you guys have a great time and catch a bunch of fish!" the old man said with a grizzled smile.

"Oh, we will!" Tim responded. "I've never been skunked yet!" They loaded their supplies onto the boat and then headed off for the IGA.

Less than an hour later, the houseboat was ready for casting off. Sol unwound the mooring ropes from the dock anchors both fore and aft, and Tim expertly maneuvered their floating, home-away-from-home out to the cove. As they began to move toward the main river channel, Sol was struck by the serenity he was feeling, and he was overwhelmed by a newly realized freedom. *I could go anywhere I choose on this river. Anywhere!* And even though it was only just after 8:oo a.m., Sol got two beers out of the fridge and brought them up to the pilot house. "We're on the Mississippi River!" he said with exuberant joy. "That deserves a drink!" Tim agreed, and as they clinked the necks of two bottles of Old Style, the two men toasted their houseboat, their rekindled friendship, and the adventure on which they were embarking together.

# CHAPTER TWENTY-SEVEN

They moved upriver, and Sol began exploring the boat. Among the papers and brochures in the living area, Sol found a pamphlet chronicling the geography and history of the Mississippi River. He read out loud: "The Mississippi River is a natural wonder. Its name is attributed to the Chippewa nation, and means 'gathering of water.' It forms the drainage basin for nearly half the land mass of the United States, from the Rocky Mountains to the west all the way to the Appalachian Mountains in the east. All in all, over 640,000 cubic feet of water are moved by the river every second. That amounts to nearly 5 million gallons of water. Every second. Put another way, that's 15 acres of land covered in water 1 foot deep, all being drained by the river every second. Wow!" he said, "That is an astounding amount of water!"

He read on. "Given its connection to so much of the expanding frontier, as well as the ready transportation afforded by the Mississippi and all the tributary rivers draining into it, it is no wonder that the Mississippi River became a main focus of settlements and trade agreements, and especially so at points of merger with other rivers. Hernando de Soto first explored the lower half of the river, making his way north as far as Memphis in 1541. The French, led by Canadian-born Louis Joliet and Father Jacques Marquette, explored and established settlements along much of the northern half in the latter part of the seventeenth century."

Tim interrupted Sol's travelogue. "And now, this river belongs to us!" Tim continued piloting the houseboat upriver, and Sol lay back on the chaise-sofa, feet up, soaking in the sun and being soothed by the calming, rocking motion of the boat as it carried its passengers over the water. He imagined what they might look like from the vantage point of the green, tree-covered bluffs high above on either side. Looking up at them, he likened them to seasoned theatregoers, observing the river scene from the loge section, distant and seemingly unaffected by the activity below. *We've seen this all before.*

After almost an hour of moving northward, Tim found a backwater area he said would be great for catching panfish and the occasional catfish. He maneuvered the boat into a likely spot, and then he cut the engine off and flipped a switch to drop the anchor. Before long, Tim had two poles rigged for himself and two for Sol, and all four lines were in the water. They caught a few crappies, as well as a dogfish, which Tim killed and threw into the shallows. "They don't call 'em dogfish for nothing," he said. "They bark at you. Awful creatures."

They moved the boat several times, seeking better fishing holes, and by mid-day, they had over thirty crappies in the live well. They decided to leave it at that, and Tim motored out onto the main channel again, heading the boat northward until they approached the lock and dam at Trempeleau. It took nearly an hour to get permission to enter the lock, and another forty-five minutes to completely make it through. The slowness of the process would ordinarily have driven Sol to distraction, but for some reason now, it didn't bother him at all. He and Tim sat talking about old times, drinking beer and snacking on cheese curds and chips. It was as though the rest of the world didn't exist.

They moved upriver another several hours before

deciding to find a place to anchor for the night. Tim steered the boat out of the channel to a quiet spot, far enough away to discourage the flies and mosquitos, but close enough to draw some protection from the bluffs if a wind were to whip up in the night. They anchored the boat and settled in.

Tim showed Sol how to scale and filet the fish; it had been thirty years since Sol had been fishing. Despite Sol's best efforts, Tim ended up cleaning over twenty. Tim then moved to the kitchen, where he breaded the filets in what he called his "secret recipe," frying them in hot oil on the stove. Their dinner consisted of crappie filets and beer, and Sol couldn't imagine wanting anything else. The stories about lead and mercury levels be damned; these fish tasted wonderful.

After supper Sol sent a quick text to Emma, promising to call her the next evening, and he opened a bottle of Glen Morangie. He offered to share it, but Tim preferred his Old Style, so they sat out on the rear deck, quietly watching as the sun began to fade and getting pleasantly inebriated. A perfect end to a perfect day.

---

In the morning, Sol woke first, so he set about making breakfast. He made a pot of coffee and began frying bacon, figuring the smell would entice Tim, which it did. "Good morning, buddy. Smells like bacon."

"Yup," Sol said, "and coffee. Eggs are almost done, and so is the toast." They sat down and ate, discussing how to plan out the remainder of the trip. Tim told Sol he had always wanted to go to a place called the Northern Palms Casino about 60 miles south of the Twin Cities. It was a resort that nurtured a Caribbean image, and some friends told him they had a great time there. "Do you think we have enough time to get that far and still get back?" Sol asked.

"I think so, but it means we do a little less fishing and a lot more boating. And maybe we get back Friday instead of Thursday. Are you game?"

Sol thought about it, but it didn't take long. "Sure, why not," he said. "We're not on a schedule. Go for it!"

And so, they did. Tim and Sol took turns piloting the boat all the rest of that day, making it almost all the way to Alma, Wisconsin, where they moored for the night, opting to wait till morning to negotiate the next lock and dam. After they finished a supper of grilled bratwurst and beer, Tim watched some television while Sol sat outside and called Emma. He couldn't wait to fill her in on all the details of his little adventure, but it rang and rang with no answer. After texting her to expect his call, he was a bit confused, and he couldn't help feeling a little nervous when she didn't answer. But he decided to simply try again later. *Maybe she just went to the store or something and left her phone in the car. No need to catastrophize...* Still, he felt as if the pit of his stomach was crawling up into his chest.

Fifteen minutes went by, and Sol phoned again. Again, no answer, but he decided to leave a message. "Emma? Hey, where are you? I texted you that I'd be calling this evening. Give me a buzz when you get this."

Fifteen more minutes passed, so Sol decided to try her home phone. No luck there, either, so he left a message on her answering machine: "I hope you're okay. I texted you that I'd be calling tonight. Maybe you didn't get the text? Well, anyway, my friend Tim and I are heading up the Mississippi. It's a great houseboat. We rented it from a guy named Sid, who looks just like you'd imagine a guy named Sid who rents houseboats would look. Caught some fish. Now we're heading up to a place Tim wanted to go. It's a casino called Northern Palms, about 60 miles south of St. Paul. We probably won't get back to La Crosse until Friday, and I'll stay the weekend with my aunt, so don't look for me until next Monday. When you get this, give me a call back, okay? Talk to you later."

What Sol had no way of knowing was that while Emma was not in her apartment (she got stuck in a horrendous traffic jam after a six-car pileup on the Eisenhower), someone else *was* there. Mike Althus had followed another tenant into the building and then picked the lock on Emma's door. He intended to wait for her to come home. He was convinced that he could make her understand; make her believe that they belonged together. All he needed was to be alone with her. He heard the message as Sol spoke it into Emma's answering machine, and an evil grin emerged on his face. *This is perfect! Mr. Clean number cruncher just gave me all the information I need to give him a big surprise. And nobody can connect Mike Althus to it. Nobody knows I heard the message. No one could suspect me!*

Of course, this meant he would have to wait to see Emma, but it would be worth it. He took a quick look out the door to find the hallway was empty. He turned the lock on the door so it would lock behind him, and he quickly slipped out the back end of the building.

———

About thirty minutes later, Emma finally made it to her apartment. She knew Sol would be calling, and when it became clear she was going to be stuck in traffic she had reached for her phone, but it wasn't in her purse. She must have left her cell in her desk drawer at work. There was nothing she could do. The traffic jam took forever to clear, and by the time she got home she was about as frustrated as a caged puppy who had to pee. Which, as a matter of fact, she did. Coming out of the bathroom she saw her phone on the kitchen counter, its message light blinking, so she pushed "answer" and listened to Sol's message. She hit "call back" and finally heard Sol's voice. "Emma?" he said, sounding more anxious than he wanted.

"Oh, Sol..." Emma was suddenly crying tears of frustration and anger.

"Emma? Are you... is everything okay?" Sol began to get even more concerned.

"No. I mean, yes. I'm fine. Nothing to worry about. It's just that I knew you were calling, and there was a huge pileup on the freeway, and I apparently left my cell in my desk so there was no way I could call you, and I finally, *finally* got home and I had to pee..." The flurry of words and the tears all whirled around, but it sounded like music in Sol's ears: Emma was okay. There was no problem. She just got stuck in traffic. That's all. Normal stuff. *No need to catastrophize.*

"Emma..." he waited for her to calm down a bit, "it's okay. Just a glitch in an otherwise normal day. Take a breath."

Something about the sound of Sol's voice was like an elixir, a calming, soothing balm cooling an overheated boiler in her head. She sat down and she did as he suggested: she took a deep breath. Two, in fact. "Okay. I'm here. I'll be fine." Another breath, then she said, "Okay. So, you're heading north."

"Yeah, it's been a great time so far. The houseboat has everything. A/C, a full kitchen, two queen beds. It even has a satellite dish and flat screen TV! Which we haven't used hardly at all, but still..."

She couldn't help smiling. He sounded like an excited little boy. So different from the formal, detached, all-business Mr. Severson she knew at the office. "Sounds great. Sorry I wasn't here for your call."

"Never mind that. Stuff happens. Traffic jams happen. You okay now?"

"Yes," she replied. "I'm home. And I got your call. And tomorrow I'll get my stupid cell phone back. And next Monday you'll be heading back home."

"Emma... I'm glad you're okay." She heard the unmistakable affection in his tone. "Thanks, Sol. Call me again if you get a chance, okay?"

"I will. Relax. Good night, Emma." He hung up the phone at the very moment he realized he was beginning to love her. *Well how do you like that?* he said to himself. And were he to have answered himself, he would have said he liked it just fine.

He rejoined Tim in the living quarters, where they watched a Bogart movie on TCM. Two scotches later, Sol was fast asleep.

# CHAPTER TWENTY-EIGHT

In the morning, Sol and Tim had to wait for a huge barge to get in and out of the lock, so they did some more fishing. They caught two walleye and a small northern, plus a decent-size carp, all of which they threw back.

They moved in closer to watch the barge move through the lock. It was quite a process, as the large towboat was pushing fifteen fully loaded flatboats, fastened three across and five deep, and all full of coal. The barge workers had to detach the front six flatboats and moor them, because the lock could not hold the full length of the barge. After securing the partial load a good distance downriver, the captain slowly maneuvered the remaining nine flatboats around and past the others, eventually positioning the barge in front of the lock. The gates opened, and as the captain pushed the load forward, Sol was amazed at the precision. There couldn't have been more than a foot or so clearance on either side as the entire, massive barge moved into the lock. Once inside, the gates were shut and the water began to flow in, raising the entire craft up to the level of the upper river channel.

The process took well over an hour just to get the first portion of the barge through. After securing the partial load, the workers disconnected the towboat and the captain moved it back into the lock to return for the other six flatboats. As he watched the process, Sol thought of his father working on just such a barge, hopping from one place to another, maneuvering the heavy steel cables and winches that secured the load. He recalled hearing that every year at least one deck hand died on the job, after a steel cable suddenly snapped or a wrench slipped or the load shifted. It occurred to Sol that this could have just as easily happened to his father; in which case, Sol might never have been born at all.

After the towboat was lowered again and was heading out to retrieve the other flatboats, the lock and dam operator let a group of small craft enter and move upriver, including Sol and Tim's houseboat. By about 10:00 a.m., they were again motoring north and west, following the great water deeper into Minnesota. A couple of eagles flew above, very high up, their bright white heads and tails unmistakable against the blue, cloudless sky.

The sojourners were tying off their boat at the Northern Palms pier by suppertime. There were dozens of boats docked there, and a real party atmosphere was already starting. As they headed up to the casino, Sol was amazed at the size of the place. He could only guess, but it looked like there might be 600 hotel rooms attached to the casino structure, and he saw signs indicating three different restaurants. The image of palm trees was everywhere, and they even had managed to grow a small grove of 25-foot-tall cocoa palm trees inside the main entrance. The trees were clearly visible through the huge glass panels forming the fascia of the main entrance, so that those approaching had the illusion of entering some sort of tropical paradise, which was no doubt the intent. On entering, they bypassed the lobby and headed for the casino area, where Tim was anxious to try his luck at the blackjack tables.

Inside, it was stimulus overload. Flashing lights, neon everywhere, buzzers and bells ringing, people in constant motion (except for those locked in close combat with their one-armed bandits); for first-time visitors like Sol, the place was mesmerizing. There was also the unusual smell of cigarette smoke and its accompanying bluish haze. It had been quite some time since Sol had been in a building where smoking was still allowed. It didn't bother him so much as it brought back memories. His parents both smoked cigarettes when Sol was young, and there was something strangely comforting for him about the smell of the smoke.

Tim got some chips and sat down at a $5 table. Sol ordered a scotch and stood by watching. Tim stood pat on an 18 hand and won. This was followed up by a dealt blackjack and a double-down option on a pair of 10s. After an hour, Tim's $50 cache of chips had grown to $120. He was feeling pretty invincible, and Sol encouraged him to take his winnings and walk away, but Tim would have none of it. Predictably, his luck turned, and he began to lose. Ninety minutes later Tim had only $25 of chips left. "That's how these places stay in business, I guess," Tim said, ruefully. They decided to head to one of the restaurants in search of supper, with Tim vowing to come back to a different table afterward and try his luck.

After an excellent hamburger and fries, they headed back to the blackjack table, where Tim spent another three hours chasing the low-stakes dragon. Sol wandered around the place, people-watching, and nursing another scotch before he settled on a seat at the nearby sports bar. He was watching a baseball game on the overhead TV when he felt someone tap him on the shoulder. He turned around and saw his brothers-in-law. Out of nowhere, here were Bobby and Jeff Larson, large as life. All the associations came flooding in on Sol in an instant: their uncomfortable presence at Jan's and Amy's funerals, the distance Jan had kept from these guys and the reasons for it, the money Jan had given to Jeff until she finally said, 'no more.'

"Sol! What in the hell are you doin' here?" Bobby spoke first, extending his hand.

Sol shook Bobby's hand followed by Jeff's, and he stammered, "I... I guess I'm just..."

"Slumming, eh?" Bobby said, laughing cynically. "Good to see you! We love this place, when we can afford it," he said. Sol thought he saw a greedy glint in Bobby's eye, which seemed to jump right into Jeff's eye, too. "I guess you must be doin' okay, eh? Just out takin' it easy? A little vacay from the humdrum life with all the ritzy folks?"

Sol began to steel himself a bit. "Yeah, just getting away for a while. How are you two?"

"Living the dream, baby. Just livin' the dream, aren't we, Jeff?"

"Oh yeah, livin' the dream. You got a room here? Maybe we could bunk in with you for a couple days... You know, catch up on old times. Or maybe you ain't alone? You find somebody to replace our dear departed sister?" *Same old Jeff.*

"Nope, sorry, I'm here with a friend, a guy I knew from high school. We rented a houseboat, but we can't stay long."

"Houseboat, eh? Cool! Hey! Maybe Bobby and me could show you some ropes on the gambling end of things. We know a few tricks, stuff the dealers don't want you to know. Maybe split the winnings with you. Whaddya say?"

Sol was becoming annoyed already, and it was not yet three minutes since they had reacquainted. "I'm not much of a gambler," Sol said.

"That's what I mean!" Jeff piped in quickly. "We could

teach you how to do it. Share some of our good knowledge with you. Just need a stake to get started with."

Sol's mind was working hard now, trying to play out the various scenarios into which this ridiculous low-rent melodrama might devolve, and how best to avoid them. *It's really only money they're after. If I give them some money, maybe they'll just go away, at least long enough for us to get out of here.* "So... what you're saying is, if I give you a starting investment, you both will split your winnings with me?" Sol said, invitingly.

"Sure! If that's how you want to do it, that'll work! You wait and see! You can get even richer than you already are, and you won't have to do a thing!"

"Okay," Sol said, peeling off two $50-dollar bills. "Here's $50 bucks each. Let me know how you're doing." The two morons looked as though they had just fleeced an unsuspecting tourist and headed off immediately to make their fortunes. Sol, in the meantime, abandoned a nearly full glass of scotch and headed directly for Tim, finding him just where he left him at the blackjack table.

"How's your luck?" Sol said, already knowing the answer by the paltry stack of chips in front of him. "Not a good night for ole Tim," came the response. "Come on, I think it's time to move on," said Sol.

As they made their way back to the pier, Tim said, "Where are we going?"

"I ran into Jan's no-good brothers, if you can believe it. And they're just as worthless as they used to be. I gave them some money to keep them busy for a while, but I want to move on before they figure out where to find me again. Let's just move downriver a ways, and then we can moor someplace for the night. We can come back again tomorrow night if you want. Okay?"

"No problem," came the response. "Hard to believe you would run into those two just out of the blue."

"Yeah, of all the gin joints in all the world…"

"Well, I guess it's probably for the best. I would have just kept losing anyway."

"Like you said, that's how these places stay in business."

They got down to the pier and cast off, moving the houseboat back out into the channel before heading southeast on the wide, darkening waters. There was a bright moon above and a cloudless sky. Sol watched the water go past, feeling the breeze cool his face, as relieved as if he'd escaped a close call with death.

They continued while the moonlight lasted. When it got too dark to navigate the river channel, they moored the boat for the night.

---

Mike Althus was making his way northwest on I-94 in a car he stole from a parking lot in Elgin. After getting out of town, he found a side street in South Beloit and exchanged license plates with a Buick parked in a driveway. In the passenger seat lay a map with the route marked and some information he'd printed out about the Northern Palms casino. In the back seat was a Marine issue assault pack which contained his pair of black combat boots, camo gear, his Steiner optics, a boot knife, a KA-BAR fixed blade, and his favorite, an Al Mar SERE combat folding knife. He had considered using a scoped rifle and just picking his target off from atop one of the bluffs along the Mississippi (he consistently qualified for Sharpshooter status while enlisted), but he finally opted for a less traceable method of killing. Besides, he had always preferred the close contact form of military assault. For Mike Althus, there was nothing quite like looking into the eyes of an enemy as you gutted him, the feel of his warm blood spurting out, seeing the terror on the man's face and his surprise as death led him away. Still, the pack also contained a Ruger SR40 and three 15-round magazines, just in case.

As the clock was approaching 4:00 a.m., Althus decided to pull off the road and get a couple hours of shut-eye. He found a rest area and stowed all his gear in the trunk away from prying eyes. But, as he locked the doors and settled back into his reclined seat, he found it hard to relax. Every time he closed his eyes, his mind was filled with the image of this Delbert guy with Emma, and Emma was *his* girl, and the fever of the kill raged inside him. Finally, he dozed, but only a little. The sun had barely climbed the first rung of the ladder when Althus was again back on the freeway, moving toward his target.

# CHAPTER TWENTY-NINE

The morning intruded on the peaceful riverboat. Tim rose first and thought he'd try catching their breakfast. He had two lines in the water before the coffee was ready, and had some difficulty getting his coffee poured, as the fish were fairly jumping onto his baited hooks, one after another. He finally pulled in both lines after landing eighteen crappies. He had them all scaled, fileted, breaded, and the first several in the pan before Sol even opened his eyes.

"Fish for breakfast?" Sol was incredulous, rubbing the sleep out of his bleary eyes.

"Nothing better!" Tim said, as he set the platter of filets on the table. Sol poured himself some coffee and considered whether to believe Tim's declaration. Before long, the fish was all consumed, along with some scrambled eggs and a pot of coffee.

They set about deciding what to do with the rest of their day, opting to return to the Northern Palms for the first part of it. Tim hoped he might at least break even. Sol didn't even bother trying to disabuse him of that unlikely notion. He was fairly certain Jeff and Bobby would not still be hanging around after they realized their meal ticket had skipped out. Still, when they got back to the Northern Palms pier at around noon and Tim headed up to rebuild his imaginary dream home, Sol opted to stay in the houseboat. No use tempting fate.

He tuned in some fishing show on the outdoors channel. *It is amazing how constantly they catch fish*, he laughed to himself, wondering how many hours of taping were necessary to get those few minutes of usable action.

He watched another show, this time about bass fishing at some tournament down in Arkansas, and somewhere in mid fish, Sol nodded off to sleep.

Over an hour passed before he was awakened by the sound of someone stepping onto the boat. "Tim, is that you? You lose everything already?" Sol said.

"Permission to come aboard, Cap'n?" Sol's countenance sank as he recognized Jeff's voice. *How the hell did they find me?* Sol wondered as he rose to meet the invading force.

"I guess you're already onboard, so permission isn't really an issue, is it?" As soon as he said it, he wished he hadn't. It was too provocative a response for these fools.

"Well, that's a fine welcome, ain't it, little brother?" Bobby looked over his shoulder at Jeff, who had emerged from behind him.

"Yeah, you'd think he wasn't happy to see us," Jeff chimed in. "And us just comin' to pay our respects and give you your share of the winnings. But I guess we could just keep it." Jeff got a stupid grin on his face, rubbing the stubble on his chin.

Sol considered the possibility that these blithering idiots might actually have gotten lucky, but he dismissed the notion outright. "So, we all got rich, huh?" Sol said. "And what's the big prize?"

"Oh, well, we sorta had to reinvest part of it, but we been watching a slot that's about to pay off huge," Bobby said. "If you want to make out big, we only need another hundred or so. Or we can give you back your part of the winnings so far. Your choice, but you'll be missing a big payoff if you don't take the chance."

Sol knew the drill. He also knew that if he didn't give

them some more money, they would never leave him in peace. He manufactured excitement and said, "That does sound like a pretty good chance. You're sure it's about to hit?" They both nodded like bobblehead dolls. "Okay, I'm in." And he handed them another hundred dollars.

"You'll see," Jeff said. "We're gonna hit the big payoff!"

They turned to leave, and Bobby stopped. "Oh yeah, I almost forgot. Your buddy up at the casino was paging you to come to the front desk. We heard it before we headed down here. That's how we knew you must've come back. So high class though!" Bobby changed his voice to imitate how he imagined an English butler might sound: "Mistuh Sevuhson. Mistuh Delbuht Sevuhson in the pier area, come to the front desk, please." They both laughed as they stepped off the boat and onto the pier.

Sol said, "Thanks. I'll be up there in a bit." And then, just to make them think he might believe their story, he added, "Don't forget to bring me my winnings!"

"We won't, Mistuh Sevuhson. We won't," Bobby said, his English butler imitation about as believable as his claims of winning. Sol could hear them as they laughed their way off the pier and back up to the casino.

Sol wondered what in the world Tim could have wanted that he would page him like that. He got his wallet and keys and secured the houseboat, and then he headed up to see what Tim needed.

---

From a far corner of the marina area, Mike Althus was doing reconnaissance. There were only a few houseboats moored in the Northern Palms marina; most of the boats were cuddy cabins or pontoon boats. But he needed to be sure which boat contained his target, and when Sol headed up to the casino, he found it. He watched as Sol headed into the main entrance, and then he sat down to formulate his plan.

---

When Sol walked into the lobby he was met by Tim, who said, "Who else knows you're up here?"

Sol replied, "Nobody except Aunt Christine and Emma. Why?"

"Because somebody paged you to come to the front desk."

"It wasn't you?" Sol asked, a furrowing brow forming across his forehead.

"No, I didn't page you," Tim replied.

"Then who..." Sol turned to inquire at the concierge station.

A bored-looking young man in a patently ridiculous Hawaiian shirt was at the desk. "How can I help, sir?"

"Somebody paged me to come up to the front desk from the pier area. My name is Sol Severson. Could you tell me who paged me?"

"Well I spoke to him, but he didn't leave any name. Except yours, that is." He chuckled like his wit had just surprised him. "But it wasn't Sol, it was something like Delwyn or-"

Sol interrupted him, "Delbert."

"Yeah! That was it! Delbert Severson!" You would have thought he just solved the Einstein problem in Euclidian geometry.

"Well, what did this guy look like?" Sol asked, a bit urgently. Sensing this might actually be important, the young man, whose name was Jason, as it turned out, said, "Oh, I never saw Delbert. He never showed up."

Sol was beginning to have a deeper appreciation for Bud Abbott. "No, Jason, I mean the guy who asked you to page me. What did he look like?"

"Oh, sorry. Yeah, that guy was pretty buff. He wasn't real tall, maybe just under 6 feet or so, and he had a sort of light-brown crew cut. Dude looked like he could do some serious damage, like he might have been in the Army or something."

Sol's skin began to feel clammy and he started to turn pale. Tim saw it right away, and he said, "You all right there, buddy? Did you see a ghost or something?"

Sol thanked young Jason for his help, and looking around nervously, he turned to find a place to sit down. "What's wrong?" asked Tim.

"The man that kid was describing sounds like Mike Althus. I have no idea how he could have found me here..." Sol felt the fear racing from his gut to his scrotum and then up his spine, seizing him with a tight-fisted grip. "Emma!" he said out loud, and he dug around frantically for his cell phone. It wasn't there. *On the boat! I must've left it on the boat!*

Sol jumped up and ran to the front door, nearly knocking over some poor guy and his young wife, and he raced down to the pier with Tim following closely behind. They got to the boat and Sol fumbled with his keys, nearly dropping them overboard as he rushed to unlock the cabin door. There was his cell on the counter beside the refrigerator. He grabbed it and entered Emma's number. It seemed to take forever to connect. One ring. Two rings. "Come ON!!!" he shouted at the phone. Three rings. Four...

"Hello? Sol?"

Sol breathed out a sigh of relief. "Emma?" He heard the panic in his own voice, and it startled him. He didn't want to panic Emma. After all, if she was now talking to him, and if Mike Althus was up here, then she was in no imminent danger. *No need to catastrophize.* He took a breath. "Where are you?"

"I'm just about to leave work. It's a little early, but I have a dentist appointment. Is something wrong? How's your trip going? Catching lots of fish?"

"Emma, I think you need to sit down," Sol said.

"Why, Sol? You're starting to scare me."

"I think you should find somewhere else to stay for a while. I'm pretty sure Mike Althus is up here, and if he is, it's not for a vacation. And no matter what happens up here, he's eventually going to be coming back to Mundelein. Is there a relative you can stay with or a friend?"

Emma heard everything Sol had said right up to the words "Mike Althus," after which she essentially heard nothing else.

"Emma? Did you hear me?" Sol said, with increasing firmness.

"Yes, Sol. What about Mike?"

"Emma, Mike is up here, he's found out where I am, and I think he's going to try something. I want you to go somewhere safe until this blows over. Do you understand?"

"Yes, Sol. I'm going to call the police."

"That's a good idea. Call that detective, what was his name?"

"Sgt. Baker," she said.

"Yeah," Sol said quickly, "call him right away. But then find someplace to stay where nobody would know to look.

I'll keep in touch but let me call you. Okay? You understand?"

"I understand, Sol. Please stay safe. Please be careful. He can be very dangerous."

"I know, Emma. Okay, I'll talk to you soon." He clicked off the phone and looked up at Tim. "We need to get out of here."

"Okay, buddy. I'm with you. Let's go."

Sol scanned the outlying areas of the marina, looking for anyone remotely resembling Mike Althus, but saw no one. They disconnected the mooring ropes and Tim moved the boat out of the harbor area. Soon they were heading downriver, and Tim hollered down, "I think we might have gotten away before he saw us leave."

But Sol never had the sense they were escaping the lion's den; in fact – quite the opposite – he couldn't shake the feeling that they were heading directly into its mouth.

# CHAPTER THIRTY

Sol and Tim motored downriver, the current helping them move faster than previously, which was good, because their only goal was to get back to La Crosse in one piece, and as quickly as possible. While Tim piloted the boat, Sol kept a watch for anything suspicious approaching from behind, and for anything that looked out of the ordinary on the bluffs and riverbanks.

Their first objective was the Lock and Dam Number 3 at Red Wing, MN. That would be the first situation in which they would be vulnerable, although any attack that might come at that time would be in full view of visitors, onlookers, other boaters, and the lock operations crew. They would also have to stop for fuel soon, which might be their most dangerous moment.

To Sol, the boat's steady progress seemed excruciatingly slow and tedious. He felt trapped. But there was nothing to be done. The boat's maximum speed was perhaps 23 miles per hour, and no amount of fretting or complaining or even praying, were he so inclined, would alter that fact. The only thing he could do was to keep a sharp eye out. There were no weapons on board with which they might defend themselves, but at least he could eliminate the element of surprise by keeping ready.

Another two hours passed before the fuel stop approached. It was a local place called the Anchor Boat and restaurant, a place that catered to boaters. It seemed to be popular; about twelve boats were docked there. After getting theirs tied off, Tim volunteered to stay with the boat as it took on fuel, while Sol went ashore to order some food. While he was waiting for their order, his phone rang. The number was unfamiliar, and he hesitated before answering, but he thought maybe it was Emma, calling from her new safe place. "Hello, Mr. Severson?" came a man's voice on the other end of the line.

"Yes, this is Sol Severson. Who is this?"

It was Sgt. Baker from Mundelein. "I got your cell number from Emma Prentiss, and I just wanted to let you know that police in Minnesota and Wisconsin and of course here in Illinois are aware of your situation, and everybody is looking for this guy. Is there any information you can give us that might help us find him?"

Sol had nothing of value to provide. He told the sergeant he had no idea how Althus knew where Sol was, or even how he knew Sol's name.

Sgt. Baker said, "We think we figured out that much. He probably got your name from running a search on your license plate. And remember that message you left on Emma's answering machine?"

"Of course, I remember," Sol said.

"We interviewed one of Emma's neighbors who thinks he saw Althus follow him into the building that day. We think he was in her apartment and heard your message on her machine." Sol shuddered to think he had given this maniac the very information he needed to find him, and that he had gotten that information by being in Emma's apartment.

Sol informed the detective about their current status and whereabouts, gave him a description of their houseboat and the name of the rental place in La Crosse, and told him of their plan to keep moving downriver. He said there had been no contact with Althus, and he didn't know if or when there might be. Sgt. Baker thanked him, and encouraged him to continue with his plan, and to keep him apprised of any new information, which Sol agreed to do. Sgt. Baker also let Sol know that Emma had found a safe place to stay, which helped Sol feel better.

After the phone conversation, Sol paid for their food and headed back to the houseboat. As he neared the boat, there was no sign of Tim. Sol called out, "Tim? Where are you at?" No response. Sol's steps toward the boat slowed to a stop. He inched forward, and he saw Tim lying on the rear deck, unmoving. "Tim!" Sol called out to him. He moved closer, looking out for any sign of Althus, when he saw a second set of legs on the rear deck of the boat. Closer still, he saw that those legs belonged to Mike Althus. Neither man was moving at all, and there was blood staining Althus' face and shirt. Tim's midsection was also bloody, but he began to stir and struggled to sit up. Sol dropped the food and jumped onto the deck to help his friend.

He propped Tim up from behind. It was clear he had been cut several times, slashing gashes that ran across his left arm and across his abdomen and upper chest. The lacerations oozed blood but seemed to not be very deep. He was gaining more awareness. "Man," he said, "he must've been hiding in one of the cargo holds. He came at me out of nowhere. I was just looking out at the river, fueling the boat."

"You're cut! How did you stop him?" Sol asked.

"Well, he came at me from behind. When I heard him, I turned around and he slashed at me with his knife. But I backed up and it barely got me on the arm. He swung it back the other way and got me a good one across my belly. But when he swung it a third time, I used his momentum to swing a full roundhouse kick to the side of his head and he went flyin'. He was starting to get up, so I grabbed a paddle and whacked him a good one. That's the last thing I remember." Tim winced in pain. "Is he dead?"

They looked at Althus' still body. "Maybe," Sol said.

"Well, you'd better tie him up good before he has a chance to get resurrected. That is one mean son-of-a-bitch."

Sol got a rope and approached Althus cautiously. The man was lying on his face, his left arm twisted awkwardly behind him and his right arm thrown upwards against the sideboard. There was blood coming out of his right ear, and there was an open gash on the back of his head. Sol made a noose and slipped it over Althus' left hand and wrist, and then quickly pulled back on his right hand, wrapping the rope tightly to bind both wrists together behind his back. He then pulled Althus' legs up and back, wrapping the rope around first one ankle and then the other before pulling his legs tight against the resisting knots that secured his wrists. He wasn't going anywhere, and if he tried, there would be more than enough time to cold cock him.

Sol looked for and found the knife Tim had described. It was wicked looking for sure, with a curved blade and a serrated spine, and it was stained with Tim's blood. Sol kicked it to Tim. "Here. The spoils of war."

Tim picked up the blade and looked at it for a minute before he passed out again.

Sol phoned 911 and asked for police and EMT help, which arrived some fifteen minutes later. He also phoned back Sgt. Baker to let him know what happened, followed by a call to Emma, who was very relieved to know Sol was okay. After he hung up the phone with Emma, and after the

EMTs took Tim away to the hospital in Pepin, and after Sol found a cheap motel room (they wouldn't let him stay on the boat, which was now a crime scene), and after the sherriff's deputy had kindly given Sol a ride to said motel, and after Sol entered his motel room and had closed and locked the door behind him, he fell down sobbing on the bed, crying such as he had never cried before in his life.

# PART FOUR: SUMMER

Then followed that beautiful season... Summer....
Filled was the air with a dreamy and magical light;
and the landscape
Lay as if new created in all the freshness of childhood.

Henry Wadsworth Longfellow, *Evangeline: A Tale of Acadie* (1847)

———————

In the depth of winter, I finally learned that within me there lay
an invincible summer.

Albert Camus, *Return to Tipasa* (1952)

# CHAPTER THIRTY-ONE

It took several days to tidy up all the details of the mess created by Mike Althus, who Tim had not, in fact, killed, but whom he had indeed mortally wounded. Tim's roundhouse kick caught Althus along the right temple, which had concussed him, but the blow with the paddle caused an acute subdural hematoma. During the time that elapsed before help arrived, he had lapsed into a coma and suffered anoxic brain injury. The likelihood, according to the police officer who told all this to Sol, was that Mike Althus would never wake up. He would very likely spend the remainder of his useless life in a persistent vegetative state, housed in a state prison hospital. *Welcome to the turnip patch, asshole*, Sol thought.

After all the information was gathered and duly considered – including that provided by Sgt. Baker regarding Emma's history with Althus – it was quickly decided by the investigating officers that what happened on the boat was done in self-defense, so no charges were warranted against Sol or Tim.

As for Tim, his wounds were serious but not life-threatening; they sewed him up and transfused him, eventually treating him prophylactically for tetanus and other opportunistic infections and sending him on his way on the third day after admission. When he and Sol finally reconnected, it was at the hospital when Sol arrived in a cab to take them both back to the houseboat. As soon as they saw one another, they embraced instinctively. Sol said, "I am so very sorry, Tim. You never signed on for any of this."

Tim stepped back and, still holding onto Sol's forearms,

he said, "No regrets. I never thought I might have to use my karate skills in a real fight, you know? It was always more about the mental discipline. But I really knew what to do. It felt good! So really, no regrets at all." Tim let go of Sol's arms, and they both turned to walk back to the hospital lobby. "How about you?" Tim said. "How are you doing?"

"Me? I'm not the one who got sliced up like a catfish fighting somebody else's fight. I feel very fortunate; pretty guilty, but very fortunate."

Tim said, "You have nothing to feel guilty about. You never asked for this fight. And if you had been there, you would have done what you could. You need to realize something." He stopped, grabbing Sol by the arm and looking him directly in the eye. "You're not a kid anymore. You don't have to feel stupid or useless or whatever if you don't want to."

The words were like stars, simultaneously shedding light on a dark place and yielding a glimpse of places beyond. He suddenly recalled Dr. O'Keefe's words again, "It's time you stopped paying your father's debts." Sol's eyes brimmed with tears, which he wiped away on his sleeve. Without another word they resumed their trip to the cab, and with that, their voyage together.

---

It took almost another two full days of boating to return to La Crosse and Sid's Houseboat Rental. Neither Sol nor Tim had much ambition to do anything but get back home, although when they moored for the night, Tim couldn't resist the opportunity to catch a few more fish. When they finally arrived back in La Crosse, Tim sidled the craft up to the pier. Sid came out to greet them, wearing the same red plaid shirt-jacket, same floppy fishing hat, and the same scruffy beard. Sol whispered to Tim, "What did he do, sleep in those clothes all week?" Tim snorted back a chuckle.

"Hey, you buccaneers! Welcome back! I heard you had a little excitement along the way. Everything okay?"

Sol answered, "Yeah, actually. In fact, everything is a lot better than okay." Tim looked at Sol with a knowing smile. They tied off the boat, which looked remarkably unscathed by the carnage that had taken place on the rear deck (thanks to some kind soul at the Anchor Bar and Restaurant, who cleaned it up while Tim and Sol were away).

Some more paperwork, a little more money for the less-than-full fuel tank, some off-loading of their gear, and they were headed back to Tomah in Sol's Honda. As they headed down the freeway, the conversation was like a tired engine needing a primer before it could restart. Finally, Tim broke the silence. "So, you wanna do this again sometime?"

Sol looked over at Tim, who had the most serious look on his face. Sol said, "Which part?" And Tim busted out laughing, followed immediately by Sol.

Finally, Tim spoke. "I'd do the whole thing again if I had to. It was worth it, getting back together with a good friend." Sol responded by extending his hand, which Tim grasped firmly. Then Tim said, "But if we can leave out the part with the psycho-killer dude, that would be cool."

They laughed together, and Sol said, "I agree entirely."

An hour or so later they arrived back at Tim's house, and after helping Tim unload his stuff, Sol was on his way back to his Aunt Christine's farm.

---

When Sol drove up to Christine's farmhouse, he was surprised to see a car with an Illinois license plate alongside the house. He stepped out of the car, and there, on the front porch, rocking like two old ladies, were Sol's two new favorite women in the world – his Aunt Christine and Emma Prentiss. Emma had found Christine's listing in the phonebook and called her. She told Christine about what had been happening, and Christine invited Emma to come up to the farm (which had secretly been Emma's wish from the start). Emma had some time-off coming at work, so she jumped at the chance. And now as Sol moved toward the porch, she jumped again, this time up from her rocking perch and into Sol's arms, hugging him like she might never let him go. "I just couldn't wait anymore," she spoke into his ear, with tears flowing.

"I'm so glad you're here," Sol said through his own moistened eyes.

"I'm so glad you're safe." And for the first time, they kissed like two people who were deeply in love.

"Hey, remember me?" Christine interrupted the romantic rendezvous. Sol went directly to Christine and hugged her just as intensely. As the embrace subsided, Christine said, "I could hardly believe what Emma told me. Are you all right?"

"Yes, I'm fine. My friend Tim took the brunt of it. He got sliced up pretty good, but he's healing and back home. It was quite a trip."

Emma had a worried look on her face. "What about Mike? Do we have to worry about him coming back?"

Sol relayed the information he got about Mike from the

policeman up in Pepin. The relief on Emma's face was palpable. "He'll never come back. Never..." The words seeped out slowly, like cold honey, and her faraway gaze softened as she began to sense the full meaning of what she had just said. She hugged Sol again, this time with tears not only of joy but relief. Emma was feeling safe – *really safe* – maybe for the first time since that horrible scene at her high school reunion back in Rockford years ago.

The three of them visited the rest of the afternoon, and by the dinner hour Emma felt like she was right at home. It was plain to see that Christine really liked Emma, and as he became aware of this fact, Sol was feeling as satisfied and happy with life and with himself as he could remember having felt in... well, maybe ever.

Sol insisted on treating Christine and Emma to a nice dinner, which was provided in Tomah by a very fine steakhouse called the Rustic Inn. When they returned to the farmhouse, a moment of awkwardness ensued regarding sleeping arrangements. Christine was, after all, Sol's aunt and in her eighties. But Christine spoke up first. "I'm sorry I didn't have time to ready the guestroom in the house, Emma, so I'm afraid you'll have to stay out in the guesthouse with Sol. There are two bedrooms there. If you need them..." she added with a mischievous smile.

Emma blushed a bit, which Sol found absolutely adorable. "Thanks, Aunt Christine. We'll manage fine," Sol said, kissing her lightly on the cheek. "Good night."

Sol and Emma walked back to the mobile home together, hand in hand, and retired for the night. They needed only the one bed.

# CHAPTER THIRTY-TWO

The morning breeze wafted a scent of corn smut through the open window beside Sol's bed, and that lovely, earthy smell combined with a faint hint of freshly brewed coffee enticed Emma's eyes open. It was early – the clock on the nightstand said 6:10 – and she looked over at the man who lay sleeping next to her. Sol lay on his right side, his back to her, softly snoring. Emma admired the neckline of his hair, which she had noticed quite some time back, though not in this same way. Beneath the close-trimmed neckline, his back was hirsute, a thing Emma had secretly wondered about. She liked a man to be hairy.

Their lovemaking the night before was as tender as Emma could have imagined, as natural and comfortable as your favorite eiderdown duvet, that one that's soft and snuggly, and it fits just right and warms just enough in all the right places.

Emma slipped out of bed quietly, and after using the bathroom, threw on a pair of shorts and a T-shirt and followed her nose outside to find the fresh coffee. In the kitchen, Christine was busily making breakfast. "Good morning!" came the greeting. "I hope you slept well?" There was that same little mischievous smile, and as their eyes met in womanly understanding, Emma blushed again, right on cue.

"Very well, thank you, Christine. Your coffee makes a good alarm clock."

"Help yourself. You can start making the biscuits if you like. The dough is all made, just need to spoon it out on the baking sheet and throw it in the oven." Emma set about her assigned task. "I assume Sol is still asleep, but I know how to fix that," Christine said. She began frying a large panful of Applewood smoked bacon, and the aroma soon filled the room, issuing forth like a siren song. "There isn't a man alive who can resist the smell of bacon frying." And sure enough, no more than ten minutes passed before Sol came wandering into the kitchen. As soon as he walked in, Christine and Emma looked at each other and started laughing.

"What did I do?" Sol asked, a bit self-consciously.

"Oh, nothing, Sol. It was just an inside girls' joke," Christine replied. "Good morning!"

"G'morning." Sol sat down beside Emma and their eyes met, provoking mutual smiles. He poured himself a cup of coffee, his mouth watering for bacon. "I guess we *are* going to have to think about heading back home," Sol said, vaguely.

"I don't know, Sol," Emma replied. "It feels pretty homey right here."

Christine brought over a platter of bacon and eggs just as the oven timer buzzed. Emma retrieved the hot biscuits from the oven. They all ate their fill and then visited some more over coffee before Emma began to clear away the dishes. Christine interrupted her, "No, no, I'll get those. I never did like people working in my kitchen. You two go take a walk or something. This'll be done in no time."

Sol and Emma took the hint and went out to the front porch. "It is really so calm and beautiful here," Emma said, "nothing like back home. I've always lived in the city. I always thought I'd go nuts out in the boonies. But I really like it here."

They walked out to the garden and took a little tour of the outbuildings before walking along the edge of the 20-

acre field behind the house, where the corn was approaching 8 feet in height. "Boy, that corn is tall!" Emma remarked. "I've been around lots of cornfields back in Illinois, but it was always driving by. I never realized..."

"Yeah, it's different when you actually stand next to it, isn't it?" Sol replied. "Corn can even get to 10 feet sometimes. Standing alongside it, you can really get a measure of things." They walked along the edge of the field, eventually reaching the road and making a circle back to the house via the end drive. They shared few words along the way. Nature's stimulus filled the time for them both; conversation would have ruined it.

As they approached the farmhouse, Christine was on the porch. "Have a nice walk?" she said, to which they responded in the affirmative. "Come up here and sit with me," Christine said. "I have something I need to talk with you about."

She poured them each some coffee from the thermal carafe she brought out in anticipation of their return. "Sol, I hope you will consider being executor of my estate."

Sol became instantly serious. "I'm flattered, of course," he said. "But I haven't been the model nephew."

"I could just leave it with my attorney as it has been," Christine replied. "But your visit and our talks this past week have changed things, a bit. Don't you think?" It was a message of reconciliation and understanding, of grace and of welcome.

Sol considered her question, and he softened – even toward himself – as he said, "I think so. Yes." He looked out over the yard and across the bean field to the nearby hills to find his answer. "Of course, I will be executor of your will, if you want me to. Just don't make it necessary for a long time, okay?"

"Every day is a gift," Christine said. "None of us has any right to lay claim to the number of gifts we receive. But I'll do my best to not hasten the inevitable. I like getting gifts." She smiled at Sol, and at Emma – whom she did, in fact, like very much, as Sol had suspected. With the business of death having been fully attended to, the very much alive threesome sat enjoying the summer day and each other's company all the way to lunchtime.

———————

After lunch, Sol and Emma went for another walk. Along the way, Emma said, "I guess I really do have to get back. I only arranged to be gone through Monday, and here it is, Saturday already."

Out of the blue, Sol said, "What if we moved here?"

Emma stopped in her tracks. *WE?* "Sol, do you realize what you're saying?"

For a moment, Sol stopped in his tracks, too, as the full meaning of his question hit him like one of Tim's roundhouse kicks. But he quickly realized that he had truly meant what he said. "Yes, I do. Emma, I love you. Will you marry me?"

Emma's thoughts quickly returned to that phone call, the one where she began to wonder if Sol might love her. Her mind raced through all that had happened and paused momentarily at the awful detour her prior engagement to Mike Althus had caused. But just as quickly, Emma was as certain as she had ever been about anything in her life: this was the man she wanted to be with. "Yes! Yes, Sol, I will! I love you, too." And they embraced and kissed, right there in the front yard, right beside the oak tree Sol's great grandfather had planted, the same tree that had shaded three generations of Delbert Solomon Seversons.

# CHAPTER THIRTY-THREE

The trip back to suburban Chicago was different this time. Sol no longer felt as though he were escaping something. His definition of life had changed. It was no longer tied up in the affluent agony of Oakton Lakes. It would take a little time, of course, and there were lots of things requiring attention, but all of it seemed good and hopeful. One thing Sol noticed was that, of all the things he had on his list to take care of (he still loved making lists), very few had anything to do with people. The house needed to be sold, several banking and personal investment issues required attention, and so forth. But except for finishing up with Dr. O'Keefe, Sol's life in Illinois had virtually no long-term, meaningful relationships at all. His awareness of this fact initially made him feel sad, but it soon just propelled him all the more toward his return to Tomah and his new life with Emma.

Sol phoned his sister, Maura, to tell her of all that had transpired. She could hardly believe his story, especially the part about what took place on the houseboat and Tim's involvement. "Karate?" she responded, incredulously. "Tim Massey?! He was such a little wimp!" But Maura was thrilled about the part of the story involving Emma. "I knew there was something special about that lady," Maura said proudly.

As for Emma, she also had things to attend to, first and foremost resigning from work. She arranged for her and Sol to spend some time back in Rockford to meet her family and to begin making preparations for their wedding. She wanted to be married in the big church in which she had been baptized and confirmed, which happened to be a

Lutheran church, just like Sol's background.

All the arrangements went like clockwork, albeit too slowly for Sol's liking. Emma wondered if their eight-year difference in age might cause concern for her family, but it didn't. Sol got on swimmingly with Emma's father, whose name was Stuart. Stuart's wife, Ellie (Emma's mother), had died some years back after a battle with breast cancer; their shared experience of losing a wife quite likely bonded Sol and Stuart together in some deeply unspoken way. Emma's sisters, Jolene (the oldest) and Jerilyn (two years younger than Emma), also were overjoyed at the prospect of this marriage.

After meeting so many of Emma's family members and friends, Sol recalled how he once strove to avoid getting entangled in all those pictures Emma had surrounding her desk back at Argenta. *Too much drama*, he used to tell himself. It was becoming increasingly apparent to Sol that he would no longer be avoiding involvement with Emma's "life" – or with his own – nor did he wish to do so. What he had learned, finally, was that avoiding the people around you does not eliminate the drama of life; rather, the scope of the drama merely narrows until you are its only subject. And that is a terribly lonely existence.

———————

The next three months yielded a whirlwind of activity for Sol and Emma, eventuating in an October wedding. The marriage was a relatively small, but lovely, celebration followed by a wonderful party. Many Argenta employees attended and were thrilled to see Sol and Emma so happy together. Sol arranged for Tim to be his Best Man, and Tim brought Sol's Aunt Christine down for the wedding, in which she participated by standing in for Emma's mother in the lighting of the Unity candle. Sol invited Angie Corrales back at St. Joseph's, and also Dr. O'Keefe, both of whom were pleased to attend the wedding.

Along the way Sol's house was sold, and he sought and was granted licensure to practice accounting in the state of Wisconsin. By mid-November, Sol and Emma were on their way to Tomah, staying initially in the mobile home on Sol's family farm until they could find a house they wanted to buy. Emma said she would have been happy to just stay there in what she referred to as "our first house," but she agreed they would want to find a place of their own, maybe in the spring.

———————

By Christmas, Christine had begun to show some signs of slowing down. She was sleeping more and more, and she had little energy to do the things that gave her joy. The last time Sol visited her was in late February. It was a cold Sunday evening with a bright, full moon shining bluish off the snowy landscape. Sol had walked over for a visit after supper, but Christine hadn't had much to say. They were sitting together in her family room, just enjoying being together, when Christine smiled at him and said, "Remember how I said every day is a gift? I think maybe my gift list is nearing the end. But I want you to know nothing ever made me happier than when you came to see me and became a part of my life again. I'm proud of the man you have become. And I bet if he could be here now, knowing all he knows now, your father would say the same thing."

"You think so?" Sol said. "He never could before. Why

now?"

Christine had a faraway look, her greying eyes seemingly fixed on a source of wisdom beyond the living room in which she and Sol were visiting. She said, "I believe time does heal all wounds, with God's help. Sometimes there isn't enough time on this side of heaven. But in the end, all our hurts – those we have suffered as well as the hurts others have suffered through us – will be addressed. What lasts is not the hurting, but the healing."

Sol took in all that Christine said, thinking deeply about her words. "Sol, I'm getting a bit tired now. I think it's time for bed." He stood up, offering to help her get ready for bed, which she declined. He kissed her on the forehead and said he would stop by in the morning and bring Emma.

"I would like that. Good night, Sol," she said, closing her eyes.

Sol headed back through the snow across the yard to the mobile home. Christine took her last breath before he arrived there.

# EPILOGUE

The funeral for Sol's Aunt Christine was a warm and wonderful celebration, carried out on one of the coldest days of that winter. It was held in the rural Norwegian Lutheran church in which she had been a member all her life, the same church which had gathered the Severson clan for over a century, and which Sol and Emma had begun attending and were planning to join. The words spoken, the hymns sung, and the stories shared – all of it together was like a warm, summer lake in which all involved were bathed and buoyed up.

The interment was in the cemetery adjacent to the church where all of Sol's ancestors were buried, and after the funeral lunch was finished and nearly all the mourners were gone, it was to that cemetery that Sol returned. It was bitterly cold, but the wind had mercifully calmed. There was a serene silence as Sol approached the graves of his family.

He stopped by the graves of Eiver and Cornelia, his great-grandparents. Next to Cornelia was a small stone for little Maybelle, and beside hers a larger stone for Christian. Moving on, Sol found the graves of his grandparents, Delbert and Helen. Next to them was their son, Arne, who died at Midway; a military plaque honored his memory there. A bit farther down and one row over was the grave of Sol's Uncle George, now reunited with Christine, whose grave had been covered already with a mound of dirt and flowers while the mourners ate their lunch. Two small stones marked the place next to George and Christine where their twin sons, Jacob and Joseph, were buried.

Sol paused at each spot, acknowledging each person

commemorated there, before finally arriving at his parents' graves. It was here that Sol took a bit more time, for he had something he needed to say. "Dad," he began, "I'm sorry you had such an angry, difficult relationship with your father. I know how tough that must have been. It wasn't fair, the way that affected you and me, but I understand now, and I want you to know I'm okay. I think Aunt Christine was right: it's the healing that lasts. Good-bye, Dad."

Just then Emma came up to join him, linking her arm with his and pulling herself close to him. Their breath joined in a mutual cloud that defied the freezing cold as they stood there quietly together. After a few moments, Emma asked, "Are you ready?"

Sol looked at her, then with one more glance at the gathering of Seversons around him there, he said, "Yes. I am ready. Let's go home." And so, they did.

# SEVERSON FAMILY

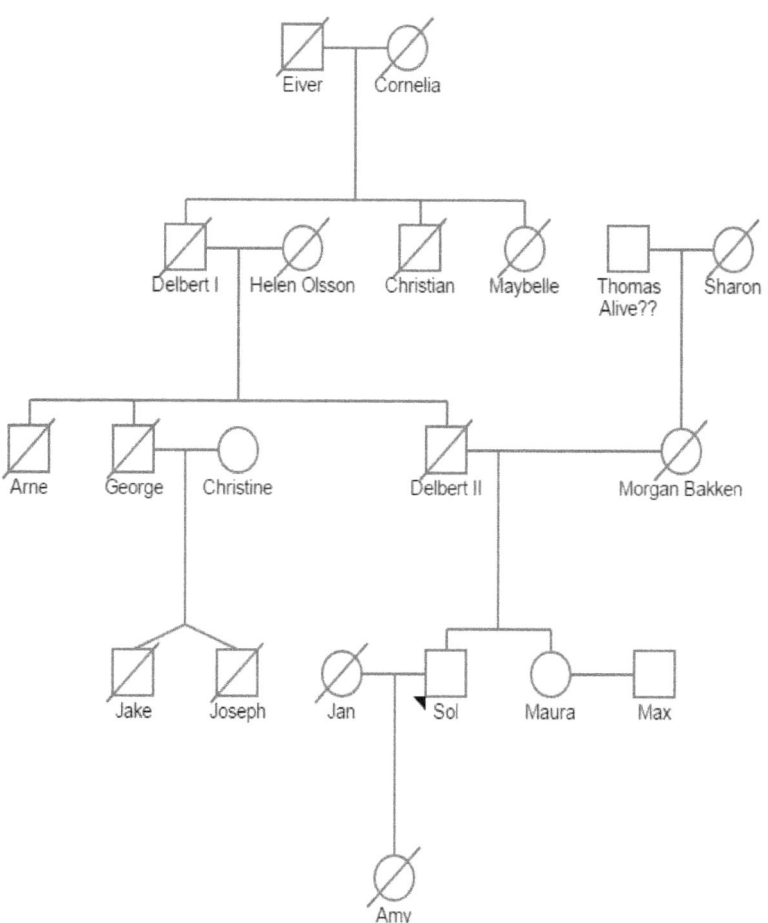

# ACKNOWLEDGMENTS

Thanks is owed to the many folks who taught, corrected, and patiently led me on the path to writing this book. Thanks to Dr. Craig Nessan, whose encouragement to write poetry led me to identify in myself the spark of writing. Thanks to the Iowa Summer Writers Festival for fueling and shaping that creative spark. Thanks for careful and skilled editing by Amy Hassinger and Sarah J. Schuster. Thanks to the forty or more persons who read the manuscript for me and offered helpful ideas for improvement.

And thanks, finally, to my wife, Susan Hansen, for loving me and tolerating my excesses.

# ABOUT ATMOSPHERE PRESS

Atmosphere Press is an independent, full-service publisher for books in genres ranging from nonfiction to fiction to poetry, with a special emphasis on being an author-friendly approach to the challenges of getting a book into the world. Learn more about what we do at atmospherepress.com.

We encourage you to check out some of Atmosphere's latest releases, which are available at Amazon.com and via order from your local bookstore:

*Interviews from the Last Days*, sci-fi poetry by Christina Loraine

*Unorthodoxy*, a novel by Joshua A.H. Harris

*Drop Dead Red*, poetry by Elizabeth Carmer

*A User Guide to the Unconscious Mind*, nonfiction by Tatiana Lukyanova

*The Sky Belongs to the Dreamers*, a picture book by J.P. Hostetler

*I Will Love You Forever and Always*, a picture book by Sarah Thomas Mariano

*Shooting Stars: A Girls Can Do Anything Book*, children's fiction by Carmen Petro

*To the Next Step: Your Guide from High School and College to The Real World*, nonfiction by Kyle Grappone

*The George Stories*, a novel by Christopher Gould

*No Home Like a Raft*, poetry by Martin Jon Porter

*Mere Being*, poetry by Barry D. Amis

*The Traveler*, a young adult novel by Jennifer Deaver

*Breathing New Life: Finding Happiness after Tragedy*, nonfiction by Bunny Leach

*Oscar the Loveable Seagull*, a picture book by Mark Johnson
*Mandated Happiness*, a novel by Clayton Tucker
*The Third Door*, a novel by Jim Williams
*The Yoga of Strength*, a novel by Andrew Marc Rowe
*They are Almost Invisible*, poetry by Elizabeth Carmer
*Let the Little Birds Sing*, a novel by Sandra Fox Murphy
*Carpenters and Catapults: A Girls Can Do Anything Book*, children's fiction by Carmen Petro
*Spots Before Stripes*, a novel by Jonathan Kumar
*Auroras over Acadia*, poetry by Paul Liebow
*Channel: How to be a Clear Channel for Inspiration by Listening, Enjoying, and Trusting Your Intuition*, nonfiction by Jessica Ang
*Gone Fishing: A Girls Can Do Anything Book*, children's fiction by Carmen Petro
*Owlfred the Owl*, a picture book by Caleb Foster
*Love Your Vibe: Using the Power of Sound to Take Command of Your Life*, nonfiction by Matt Omo
*Transcendence*, poetry and images by Vincent Bahar Towliat
*Leaving the Ladder: An Ex-Corporate Girl's Guide from the Rat Race to Fulfilment*, nonfiction by Lynda Bayada
*Adrift*, poems by Kristy Peloquin
*Letting Nicki Go: A Mother's Journey through Her Daughter's Cancer*, nonfiction by Bunny Leach
*Time Do Not Stop*, poems by William Guest
*Dear Old Dogs*, a novella by Gwen Head
*Bello the Cello*, a picture book by Dennis Mathew
*How Not to Sell: A Sales Survival Guide*, nonfiction by Rashad Daoudi
*Ghost Sentence*, poems by Mary Flanagan
*That Scarlett Bacon*, a picture book by Mark Johnson

# ABOUT THE AUTHOR

 Kurt Hansen was born in Racine, Wisconsin, and has lived in Kansas, Texas, and Iowa. He has years of experience in mental health and family systems as well as in parish ministry and administration. He holds degrees in psychology, social work, and divinity. Kurt now lives in Dubuque, Iowa, with his wife of over forty years, Dr. Susan Hansen, a professor of international business management.

9 781646 068418